THE SACRAMENT

ALSO BY OLAF OLAFSSON

NOVELS

Absolution (1994)
The Journey Home (2000)
Walking into the Night (2003)
Restoration (2012)
One Station Away (2017)

SHORT STORIES

Valentines (2007)

THE
SACRAMENT

A NOVEL

OLAF OLAFSSON

An Imprint of HarperCollins*Publishers*

Many thanks to Lorenza Garcia for her invaluable assistance when writing this book.

THE SACRAMENT. Copyright © 2019 by Double O Investment Corp. All rights reserved. Printed in the United States of America. No part of this book may be used or reproduced in any manner whatsoever without written permission except in the case of brief quotations embodied in critical articles and reviews. For information, address HarperCollins Publishers, 195 Broadway, New York, NY 10007.

HarperCollins books may be purchased for educational, business, or sales promotional use. For information, please email the Special Markets Department at SPsales@harpercollins.com.

FIRST EDITION

Designed by Michelle Crowe

Library of Congress Cataloging-in-Publication Data has been applied for.

ISBN 978-0-06-289987-3

19 20 21 22 23   LSC   10 9 8 7 6 5 4 3 2

THE SACRAMENT

HE HAD COMMITTED A CRIME. WHILE THEY WERE knitting he had allowed his mind to wander. He liked to let his thoughts drift to distant places, where there was no sadness and the nights were filled with pleasant dreams. Sometimes he would travel to the farm where he had spent the summer before last, to the barn, where he threw himself onto the hay, or to the stream, where brook trout hid beneath the banks. Sometimes he would lose himself in the comic books his father brought back from his voyages. But he never let his thoughts take him to the hospital or the cemetery.

She had snatched the knitting from him and ordered him to place his palms facedown on the table. His hands trembled slightly, but of course he obeyed. The other children pretended to be absorbed in their own work, but he could feel their eyes watching him, and her as she loomed over him.

Still you insist upon sullying yourself in the eyes of the Lord, she said, unraveling his work, the first tentative rows of a scarf. And what is this mess supposed to be?

Assuming she didn't expect him to reply, the boy remained silent. But she repeated the question, hissing this time:

What is it?

A scarf.

She scoffed, holding the tangled wool aloft for the other children to see.

Look at this scarf! Who wants to try it on?

Too terrified not to humor her, the children gave nervous, stifled laughs. Save for her class favorites, two girls who chortled out loud.

Clasping one of the knitting needles, she pressed it into the back of his right hand.

Why did our Savior suffer on the cross? Why? He suffered for you. They drove nails into his hands, like this . . . That is how he saved you. And what do you do to repay him? You belittle him. You shame his memory.

With each emphasis, she dug the needle harder into his hand. Tears pricked his eyes, but he dared not make a sound. When at last she fell silent, she waited a few seconds, which seemed to him like an eternity, before pulling the needle back and ordering him to stand up. He followed her into the corridor where she unlocked the broom cupboard and pushed him inside. He heard the key turn, and then her footsteps receding.

He knew the cupboard well. It was where they kept buckets and mops, detergent and cleaning cloths, as well as salt for de-icing the sidewalks. Once, he had used an upturned bucket as a seat, which had earned him further chastisement when she finally opened the door. And so, this time he decided to stand and gaze out the window high on the wall, a tiny window that looked out on the church. He rubbed his sore hand, where the needle had left a red indentation, but no blood.

The sky was thick with clouds, and soon it started to snow. They were small flakes that took so long to find their way to the ground that he wondered if they had gotten lost. He followed their descent, moving closer to the window to see if any of them had made it all the way. Standing on tiptoes, he could see across the yard to the fence between the school and the church, and up to the gray, flat-topped tower. He soon grew tired of craning his neck and gave in to the temptation to turn over one of the buckets and climb on top of it.

That was when he noticed something moving in the open window at the top of the tower. His rubbed his eyes and saw to his amazement that Batman himself had suddenly appeared in all his glory. His hero surveyed the city then turned toward him, as though aware of his exact location, giving the boy a meaningful, reassuring look.

Batman would save him, just as he had so often in the past, and together they would set off on an adventure, down streets and alleyways, to the harbor and out over the city—ready to assist anyone who might be in distress.

The boy held his breath as his friend took to the air. Bracing his elbows on the sill, he lifted himself up to watch the dark figure swoop down from the tower, wings flapping. For a moment, he felt a surge of hope, as well as the thrill of confirmation, for he had always feared that Batman existed only in his comic books and his imagination. But then, in the blink of an eye, his hopes were dashed, as his hero's wings appeared to falter, and he flipped over and plummeted, landing on the turf with a dull thud. For a while, the boy stared at the body on the snowy ground, slowly realizing that his hero had inexplicably transformed into Father August Frans, or rather a dark heap who only a stone's throw away showed no sign of life.

I DO NOT SPEAK WITH THE TONGUES OF ANGELS, NOR have my prayers ever moved mountains. Mysteries have revealed themselves to me, not in mirrors or riddles, but face-to-face, and neither God nor man will forgive me my sins. That which is already in ruins cannot be conquered, but rather it buries itself in the soul where it awaits its time. And yet, despite everything, I still cling to the belief that if I do not have love, I am nothing.

I won't deny that working in the garden is becoming more difficult as the years go by. But I cannot complain, because each moment is a gift from God, and except for a touch of arthritis, and the occasional bout of tachycardia, I enjoy perfect health. I refuse to impose fewer demands on myself and have no intention of reducing my workload or carrying out less onerous tasks here at the convent. When I got out of bed this morning to attend Lauds, as I stood over the washbasin in my cell, I contemplated my hands at length. All at once, they appeared alien to me, bulging veins, gnarled, like the rugosa rose I have lately been trying to nurture. It took such a battering last winter that for a while I feared it might not survive. I am more hopeful now, although it is still too early to claim victory.

My mind revisits the past, calming as night falls and the wind dies down, and occasionally I find solace in prayer. The path to truth lies amid the long winding passageways of the soul, where fear and hope do battle with each other. I have lost my way in the darkness, I have given up hope and been plunged into despair. And yet I have also walked in fields of joy, amid birdsong and the brightest of sunshine.

I slept fitfully last night. I got up twice and went over to the window, where I looked out at the garden and the fields beyond, to the mountains that surround our valley. On the second occasion, the moon broke through the clouds, casting a bluish light, so that I could see the shape of our garden clearly from my window. I never tire of contemplating it, marveling at the ingenuity of its design, the hard work put into every part of it by the generations: the rows of vegetables nearest to the convent, the stand of trees between the parterre and the ornamental garden, the berry path leading to the orchard, and of course, the orchard itself. And yet during all the years I have lived here, it is in the rose garden where I have spent most of my time, and that is where I feel the happiest.

I recognized his handwriting at once. It still looks so refined, seemingly unaffected by his age. Nowhere had his attention lapsed or his hand faltered. Each letter beautifully drawn, connecting effortlessly with those that precede and follow, forming a perfect whole, the spaces between the words oases of calm. Every line perfectly straight on the clean white paper, the blue ink like a cloudless sky. It saddens me that his handwriting should have aroused such fear in me, even before I began reading the letter.

". . . I have received a missive, which it is essential I discuss with you in person. I shall travel to the parish in a week's time and have already informed Sister Marie Agnès, who is expecting my arrival . . ."

The garden gives way to fields, and at the far end of the valley are two farmsteads, which have been there for as long as the convent. They are too far away for me to see them from my window in the moonlight, but the tractor which one of the farmers abandoned yesterday at the edge of the field is still there. I think it must have broken down, because on my way to Nones I heard a loud bang in the distance followed by silence. Occasionally, we borrow the tractor, and one of my jobs is to drive it and then to return it to the farmer. It may sound strange, but I always look forward to those days. I also like to watch the farmer bouncing through the field on it, sometimes pulling a plow or a cart, sometimes nothing, slow but sure, in all weathers, although in my mind's eye I always imagine the tractor in bright sunlight. It seems joined to the earth, part of Creation, and indeed the years have left their mark on it. I confess I feel anxious about the tractor and am afraid that this breakdown might be the beginning of the end.

When I finished reading the letter, I didn't put it down, but rather clasped it in both hands, waiting for my heartbeat to slow. I had taken it with me into the rose garden to read during the midday lull, contemplating the delicate handwriting, before placing it back in the envelope. I stood in the hot sun, listening to the birds, to the murmur of the well, yet all I could see was the snow surrounding the dark church, the schoolhouse next to it, the body on the ground. And across the bay, looming through the afternoon snowfall, Mount Esja.

Qui in tenebris et in umbra mortis sedent, I repeat day in day out, week after week, year after year. God's mercy allows the sun to rise and illuminate those who dwell in darkness, in the shadow of death . . . *He no longer has any power over me*, I tell myself. *He cannot take from me what I have already lost. I must be strong, I mustn't be afraid of him.* His silver tongue, his elegant handwriting. His words that hang in the air.

I try not to blame anyone, and mostly I have no regrets. Not about love at least.

I contemplate my hands then lean over the basin to splash my face with cold water. Last spring, we found a puppy in the garden, a skinny, forlorn little thing, barely able to walk. Sister Marie Joseph and I carried him into the kitchen, fed him warm milk, and made him as comfortable as we could. The farmers knew nothing about him, and after an intense discussion, we decided to keep him. As I argued most in favor, the Mother Superior, Sister Marie Agnès, agreed on the condition that I look after him. I have done so gladly and have become as attached to him as he is to me. I had been listening to some old records that day, which may explain how I got the idea of naming him George Harrison after my favorite Beatle. There is a resemblance, particularly to the way Mr. Harrison looked in the late '60s when they all grew a beard and long hair. The name has stuck, and now I couldn't imagine calling him anything else. He sleeps in the alcove by the kitchen door, wakes up as soon as he hears me approach in the morning, then wags his tail and waits for me to scratch him behind his ears.

Dawn breaks as I kneel in the chapel saying my morning prayers. I know where the sun seeps in through the windows and I choose my spot accordingly; I am aware of the light on my face although my eyes are closed. *Deliver me from the hand of my enemies*, I intone in silence, *so that I might serve you without fear* . . .

When prayers are over, I have a cup of coffee in the kitchen, and then George Harrison and I go for stroll in the rose garden.

Faith, hope, and love. But for me, perhaps, only love.

HE ARRIVED AHEAD OF SCHEDULE. SISTER MARIE Joseph and I had been mending fruit baskets in the shed all morning, making good progress, even though my mind was elsewhere. For as long as the oldest nuns can remember, Sister Clemence has overseen the orchards and related matters, but with the afflictions of old age she is unable to carry on. Truth be told, she should have stopped two years ago, when she was diagnosed with Parkinson's, but she dug in her heels. Of course, I understand: it is never easy to admit defeat, even at God's hands. However, last winter, she quickly went downhill. She has difficulty walking and has recently been forced to move to the ground floor. Naturally, this is hard for her, for she had grown very attached to her cell, and to the view from there across the valley.

Sister Marie Joseph and I had to unravel her feeble attempts to patch up the holes and start afresh. We only had a few baskets left to do when one of the younger nuns came to tell me that the cardinal was waiting for me in the library. She was clearly in awe, but kept from inquiring about the reason for his visit. I looked at my watch: he was almost an hour early.

I paused before the door, taking a deep breath. Although neither of them spoke in loud voices, I could hear his and Sister Marie

Agnès's somewhat hushed tones, for a deep silence permeates the convent, especially when we are carrying out our chores midmorning. At last, I grasped the handle and knocked gently as I pushed open the door.

When he rose to greet me, I could see that he had aged. Although he's only a few years my senior, I always think of him as belonging to another generation. He has a small, slender build, and a pale complexion, and he holds his head slightly forward, as if he were on the alert. I've never been able to decide whether his eyes are green or blue, and his gaze is alternately serene or piercing, occasionally both. He was never a muscular man, but now he seemed even thinner, shrunken. I noticed the silver-handled cane propped against the chair. He didn't reach for it as he stood up, nor did he walk toward me, but rather waited for me to come to him and greet him. His handshake was as I remembered, so limp it was like clutching air.

I sat down beside Sister Marie Agnès, opposite Cardinal Raffin, his back turned to the windows, which reach almost up to the ceiling, and his face south. A single cloud floated past but didn't block the sun. I was surprised at how fast it moved, because I hadn't noticed the slightest breeze out in the garden.

I was hoping that His Eminence would lunch with us, said Sister Marie Agnès, but he cannot stay long.

Yes, alas, duty calls, he said.

He and the Mother Superior have known each other since he was a young priest at Saint-Amand-Montrond, and she a simple nun here at the convent, and she sat with us longer than I had anticipated. She is both naturally talkative and eloquent, and they reminisced about old times; she shared with him the news from the countryside, to which he listened politely, asked his advice on this or that—matters about which he doubtless knew very little. Naturally, she brought up the subject of the convent's maintenance, how difficult it was, and made special mention of the chapel. He nodded, a sympathetic look on his face, and blamed a lack of funds.

What about volunteers? he asked.

They are fewer and fewer in number, she replied.

Like us, Sister Marie Agnès, he said. Like us.

I noticed that he hadn't lost his ability to speak to people as if he were standing in their shoes, and yet at the same time superior. His voice was just as I remembered, so soothing that sometimes only when he had finished speaking did the implication of his words become clear. Especially when he was issuing a threat.

I listened in silence, observing him discreetly. There he sat, the master of my fate, waiting for the opportunity to speak to me alone, once more. He was careful not to appear impatient, yet I could tell he was waiting for the Mother Superior to leave. His replies were concise without being brusque, and he asked few questions.

For years, I had tried to convince myself that he couldn't hurt me, and now, at last here was the proof, for I no longer felt afraid of him. I was free. I no longer felt the need to please him and was amazed to find that I couldn't wait to tell him so.

And this was what I intended to do, when Sister Marie Agnès finally rose from her chair and walked over to the door. We watched her in silence, and only when the door had closed did we turn to face each other. He leaned forward in his chair, brushing a piece of invisible fluff from his cowl.

I stopped off at my old church in Saint-Amand this morning, he began. I didn't announce my arrival, but simply sat and watched from a pew at the back. People came and went, mostly old folk like us, praying to their God. The young priest . . .

Father Minnerath, I said.

That's right, Minnerath. He reminded me of myself when I was his age. Determined . . .

He takes a great interest in his parishioners, I said. And he cares for those less fortunate: prisoners, drug addicts, teenage mothers, immigrants . . .

He glanced at me, then said in an impassive voice:

And you care for your rose garden, Sister Johanna Marie.

There was a time when those words would have stung me, but not anymore. I had worked with both Father Minnerath and his predecessor, although I saw no reason to mention this to Cardinal Raffin. Besides, I expected he already knew.

Yes, I said, and I care for the rose garden.

He tilted his head to one side, then, reaching into a black brief-case on the table next to his chair, he retrieved an envelope.

The only reason I came here is because this letter is addressed to you.

He handed me the envelope, adding:

I assume you can still read Icelandic.

I tried hard to conceal it, but the mere mention of the word *Icelandic* knocked me sideways. My heart started to hammer in my chest, and I felt so faint that I could barely take the letter out of the envelope.

Did he see my mask slip? I don't know. I gave it no thought. At that moment, he no longer mattered.

The letter was short, less than half a page, printed and signed in black ink. The date was also handwritten as if he had waited to send it: May 7, 2009. I read it slowly and didn't look up until I had finished. I folded the piece of paper then unfolded it again, contemplating the words.

I take it you remember him.

Yes, I said.

Unnar Grétarsson. What role did he play?

His choice of words didn't surprise me; Father Raffin often spoke in that way.

Unnar is the boy who was locked in the broom cupboard and forgotten, I replied clearly, although I doubted that Raffin needed reminding.

He sent the letter to the bishop of Iceland, who forwarded it. Obviously, I had it translated so that I could understand it, even though strictly speaking the letter is addressed to you.

I nodded. He settled back in his chair.

He saw everything, I said, more to myself than to Raffin.

The cardinal observed me in silence, and when he spoke again, he had changed his tone subtly, to remind me of his position.

As you are aware, for a long time it has fallen to me to investigate such matters, alas. In my opinion, the man has nothing new to say. Time plays tricks on the mind, and memories are capricious. He was a mere child—although, naturally, my heart goes out to him.

I scanned the letter once more, looking for the sentence.

"I didn't tell you everything . . ."

Children have vivid imaginations, Raffin said. I recalled his statement. Batman . . . the boy's upbringing had been difficult, and who knows how things have gone for him since. Who knows where life has taken him.

I found him purely by chance, I said. In the broom cupboard.

Without replying, the cardinal reached once more for his briefcase, took out a thin folder, and handed it to me.

The report you wrote back then. I've skimmed through it.

I'm afraid that as things stand, I see no alternative but to deal with the matter. And he will only talk to you.

Couldn't we do this over the telephone? I felt like saying. *Is it necessary for me to travel all the way to Iceland?* And yet I knew there was no other way.

My heartbeat had slowed, but I still felt faint and had as much difficulty rising from my chair as the cardinal did. Years ago, I had come here seeking refuge. Slowly but surely, time has come to my aid, time and the rose garden, and the days that passed like clockwork, the mountains and fields that blossomed and withered. And more recently: George Harrison.

But now that peace was shattered, and as I watched the cardinal climb into the car that was waiting for him outside, I felt as if the woman who had lived here for thirty years suddenly no longer existed.

THE STATION AT SAINT-AMAND-MONTROND IS QUIET and unassuming. Only five of us await the Paris train, and I was one of the first to arrive. Having bought my ticket in advance, I sat down on the bench on the platform, Sister Marie Joseph standing next to me, stealing a glance at her cell phone. From here you can see along the tracks as far as the mill, where they turn eastward before disappearing into a copse. Yesterday it rained, but today is overcast, and quite chilly for this time of year. I made sure to bring a shawl with me and have wrapped it around my neck and shoulders.

Sister Marie Joseph drove me here in the Renault. It's a bit of an old wreck, probably reaching the end of its days. Apart from myself, Sister Marie Joseph is the only nun who has a driver's license, a fact which I suspect makes her feel rather proud. I taught her myself, but I can't have been a very good instructor, as everybody agrees that she's a terrible driver. She has great difficulty coordinating her hands and feet when changing gear, and on top of that frequently forgets to pay attention to the traffic around her. She is an excitable, chatty person, and her mind often strays from the things she should be focusing on, namely the car and the road. That is what happened this morning when she started asking me about Iceland, and my careful replies did nothing to deter her.

The glaciers are magnificent, aren't they? Can you see them from Reykjavík? And aren't the waterfalls and hot springs splendid? Did you take many trips when you were there? Are you planning any this time? Only three hundred thousand inhabitants, amazing! And most of them Protestants . . . What made you learn Icelandic in the first place?

And so she prattled on, grilling me in the same way she had about my years as a missionary in Africa, while I kept my eyes on the road, ready to grasp the steering wheel at a moment's notice. Mercifully, there was light traffic, and she was driving more slowly than usual. I muttered something about the glaciers and waterfalls and responded to her questions about the Catholics in Iceland—who are only ten thousand in number.

Then I see why they need all the support they can get, she said. Do you think there's a rose garden next to the church?

The only explanation I had given her for my trip was that I'd been asked to fill in for someone on sick leave, telling her the church was shorthanded since the Order of the Sisters of Saint Joseph had moved out of the country after having been there for over a hundred years. Of course, this was only partly true, but I didn't have much of a choice. Even so, I felt bad and was tempted to tell her more, but fortunately stopped myself. Sister Marie Joseph is so young and naive—I was going to say simpleminded—that sometimes I worry about her. By this I do not mean that she is stupid. On the contrary, I would go so far as to say that she's in many ways highly gifted, her university degree being proof of her intellectual capacity. She is also blessed with a pure, beautiful soul, and a kind, loving nature. And yet I worry about her, the same way I worry about my roses, which are in need of constant care and attention.

I think of myself when I was her age. At first blush, we seem unalike in every way, but a closer look reveals that's not so clear. Maybe she isn't as self-assured as she pretends to be. Maybe she is still searching, despite speaking as one who has never experienced doubt, who has always felt close to our Savior and never questioned her faith. Perhaps there is something beneath the polished surface which I haven't yet put my finger on.

After parking the car, she insisted on carrying my suitcase for me, although I was perfectly capable of handling it myself, as there aren't many stairs up to the platform. She embraces me before I climb aboard the half-empty train, waving and smiling as we pull out of the station. I see her recede into the distance, and the Renault as well as it awaits her in the parking lot. It is the only vehicle there, and I begin to worry that she won't be able to start the engine, or that she will run into self-imposed difficulties on her way home. Of course, these are foolish notions, and I tell myself that it is just my nerves acting up.

The journey takes approximately three hours and the views from the train are splendid, partially at least. This is the only direct train to Paris today; otherwise I would have had to change at Vierzon Ville. I am really in no hurry, as my flight doesn't leave until late in the evening, at eleven o'clock, to be precise. I will have plenty of time on my hands once I get to Paris, and indeed, as Sister Marie Joseph pointed out, it would be ideal for me to spend the afternoon in the city, before setting out for the airport. Her suggestions made it obvious that she has never lived in Paris, only been there as a tourist, and, of course, read about it. She mentioned the main museums, and other famous attractions, although, as one would expect, churches were foremost in her mind.

Obviously, Notre Dame, she said, although personally I find Saint-Gervais particularly beautiful. More so than the Sacré-Coeur, for example—though of course that is also very beautiful, she added, as if she thought it inappropriate of her to compare God's houses. Perhaps because of the ivy, she went on, or the strains of the old organ . . .

Thus, she had chattered on, and I must admit that I felt quite relieved when we arrived at the station. While she was helping me purchase my ticket online back at the convent, I told her I hadn't been to Paris for years but failed to mention that I had lived there.

The landscape is in no way majestic, but even so I enjoy looking out the window, at the fields stretching away as far as the eye can see, and the tiny villages appearing here and there. Occasionally, I glimpse an old palace or church perched on top of a hill, or a splendid bridge crossing a river or canal. Rather than disturbing one's thoughts, if anything the scenery has a numbing effect, and before long many of the passengers have indeed dozed off.

Half an hour into the journey, I open my bag and take out the report Cardinal Raffin left behind when he visited me the other day. So far, I have been unable to bring myself to look at it, leaving it untouched on the small writing desk in my cell. However, I no longer have any excuse, so I reach for my glasses, preparing to dredge up the words I had managed with difficulty to compose on a borrowed typewriter more than twenty years ago.

ONLY WHEN I ENCOUNTERED THE DEVIL DID I REALIZE that God must exist.

For mountains to stand out there must be plains, and without darkness there is no light. For years, I had been desperate to find God, to discover for myself that he existed, for other people's assurances and obscure symbols meant nothing to me. I felt closer to him when I prayed, and despite often groping in the dark, I could sense he was near. Sometimes, I only needed a glimmer of light to show me the way, a small sign that I was on the right path. At other times, I felt so close to him that my fingertips trembled as I reached out to him. I always felt bitterly disappointed when I found myself clutching at air.

God did not loom large in my childhood home. I was born during the last days of the war, in a small village near Lyon. I was christened Pauline, after an aunt who died young. Pauline Reyer. My father was a teacher, my mother a housewife, and although my sister and I were taught the appropriate prayers, passages, and psalms, my parents were not keen churchgoers, and the Bible was only brought out on religious holidays. Even so, they instinctively followed Christ's teachings, which my sister, Madeleine, and I naturally picked up on. The two of us followed different paths when we grew up; like father, she studied to be a teacher, while I went to Paris to read theology at the Sorbonne.

My parents weren't expecting me to devote my life to religious contemplation, and my decision took them by surprise. Not that they tried to dissuade me, but when we were alone, my mother asked me what had encouraged this choice. She asked because she cared, but also because she was a little worried. I can still see us in the kitchen now. It was late afternoon and I was helping her prepare *quenelles de brochet*, having just added the cream to the chicken stock.

Has Father Bernard influenced you, Pauline?

No, I said.

And yet you meet with him regularly.

Not anymore. This is *my* decision.

We were standing at the stove together, and she turned to look at me, as if to satisfy herself that I was telling the truth.

Naturally, we'll support your decision, she said, although I can't imagine what a young woman like you is planning to do with a theology degree.

I remember an immense feeling of relief. Not because she had given me her blessing, but because for a moment I had feared that she'd been able to read my thoughts. As I stood next to her, avoiding her gaze, I felt so afraid that I started to whisk furiously to hide how much my hands were shaking.

It took me a long time to realize that I was different from other girls. Many years. Of course, I found it strange that as a teenager I had no interest in boys, especially as my friends spoke of little else, even though it wasn't all that long since we had found them all rather unbearable. Their change of heart surprised me more than my own indifference. At first, I tried to ignore my feelings, and when that failed I began to despair. It felt as if I was suffering from a disease, which I couldn't get rid of no matter how hard I tried, a terrible disease, a chancre of the soul. I certainly couldn't go to the doctor or discuss it with friends or family. People like me were only ever referred to obliquely at home, and my parents made their attitude quite clear.

I tried to inform myself, but it wasn't easy finding books on the subject in the local library. I didn't know where to look and I had to be careful no one saw me taking off the shelves works I thought might be instructive. After several trips, I ended up finding enough material to satisfy my curiosity, and to shine a dim light on my condition, although I was no closer to understanding why my soul had strayed.

Among other things, I discovered that it was against the law for people like me to pursue their inclinations until they were twenty-one. Obviously, I was horrified to learn that not only were my feelings inappropriate, they were also unlawful, and things didn't improve when early in 1960 sanctions against same-sex relations were made harsher. I remember coming home from school and seeing the front-page headline in the newspaper, which my father had left on the kitchen table. The article appeared at the bottom, but my father had folded the newspaper in such a way that it was the first thing I saw. Two thoughts occurred to me simultaneously: that he had left it like that on purpose, and that those in power must have discovered something new and terrible about people like me.

I was so absorbed by this article, which I read with a lump in my throat, that I didn't notice Madeleine until she was leaning over my shoulder.

You aren't reading about those deviants, are you, Pauline?

I gave a start and tossed the paper aside.

I was just browsing.

Monsieur Hellard is one of them.

What? I said. Monsieur Hellard came from a wealthy family and lived in a big manor house outside the village.

That's why he isn't married, and why no one will work for him.

I hardly ever heard Monsieur Hellard's name mentioned, and I knew nothing of his problems with hiring staff. I only ever cycled past his house in summer, when we went swimming in the lakes beyond, and yet now that I thought about it, I could see that the house was somewhat in disrepair, and that the windows needed painting.

But I've seen a servant working in his garden, I said.

He . . .

Isn't he a servant?

Madeleine didn't reply, but sighed softly, as though she had realized there was no point in discussing the matter with her little sister.

I must emphasize that Madeleine had a sweet nature and was kind and considerate to everyone. I had never heard her speak ill of people, which is why her remarks about Monsieur Hellard took me by surprise. Especially as there was no trace of malice in her voice, but rather compassion and sadness, as when one speaks of the dying.

It was after this that my search for God began, for I believed that in him I would find the answers to the questions that plagued me. I wasn't accustomed to going to confession, but I started visiting Father Bernard, a man in his forties with a ready smile, who had delivered a beautiful funeral service when my grandmother passed away. I didn't go straight to the heart of the matter—that took time—and never quite admitted that I was talking about my-self. However, Father Bernard was no fool, and when I attempted to broach the subject, rather than question me directly, he was content to answer my general inquiries about human nature and desire.

Finally, I took the plunge and asked him the question that had been plaguing my nights for months on end: How could God make people like that if he disapproved of such feelings?

He was taken by surprise. I could hear him stirring in his seat behind the grille and thought I saw him lower his head. At last, he seemed to find the answer, and, clearing his throat, he sat up straight.

To overcome evil in the world, we must first overcome the evil within ourselves, he said. God knew this when he created man. He knew that he could not send him unarmed to fight against evil. With each inner battle the armor forged in our soul grows stronger. Our weapon in this battle is God's kindness. But with-out that armor we stand exposed.

The evil within ourselves . . . That night I cried myself to sleep, and the next day I didn't trust myself to go to school. I had the impression that I was damned, even though all I had done was to be as God made me, and as I lay in bed staring up at the ceiling, I saw no difference between God's justice and man's injustice.

I did not declare war on him. Not then. I felt too confused, too weak. But I stopped going to confession, and during the weeks that followed, I avoided Father Bernard and didn't go to church, even refusing to attend Easter Vigil, much to my parents' surprise. Still, they didn't question me or try to persuade me to go.

Instead, one fine morning, I set off from the village toward Monsieur Hellard's house. It was a twenty-minute bike ride, and the views from the winding country road were pretty—rolling hills, vineyards, and animals grazing in the fields. Even though I cycled slowly, my heart was pounding. More than once I stopped to look over my shoulder, perhaps to make sure that no one was following me, or because I was tempted to turn back. But I carried on, dismounting just before I arrived, and wheeling my bike along the final stretch, toward a stand of trees, where I would be able to observe the house without being seen.

It looked smaller than I remembered. Not that so many years had gone by since I last saw it; indeed I had cycled past only the previous fall, after our last outing to the lakes. It was cooler now, May having barely started, the trees were in bud, and there was an acrid smell from the dead leaves composting on the ground.

I was warm after my bike ride, but soon the air felt chilly. I buttoned my cape and wrapped my scarf about my neck. There were no signs of life outside the house, or in the windows, but still I waited, as if for a sign or, perhaps, a revelation.

After a good while, my wish came true. A door at the side of the house opened, and two men emerged. One looked quite old, the other perhaps in his sixties. The older man was dressed in a thick coat, rubber boots, and a hat. He seemed unsteady on his feet, and yet he ambled about the garden, looking at the trees and shrubs, every now and then stooping to pick up a twig. Then he paused, glanced back at the house and the yard, at the sky above, the road going past the house and the copse where I was standing.

I gave a start, although I knew he hadn't seen me among the trees. Instinctively I looked away, then, collecting myself, I continued to observe him contemplating his garden and the arrival of spring. There was a remarkable serenity about him, and nothing to suggest that the devil had his claws in him.

At last, he turned around and started back toward the side door. But then he stopped in his tracks, as if suddenly the path back had grown longer, as if he had realized that he'd come too far. For a moment, he seemed to despair, unsure which foot to put first, but then the man I had thought was his servant approached, took him by the arm, and helped him to advance. And so, one step at a time, they made their way toward the door, hands clasped, palms joined in a loving gesture. Their affection for each other was clear, the consideration, the bond between them: it was as if they weren't separate entities, but rather that God had created them as a whole.

God, I say . . . I should point out that at this stage I still wasn't convinced of his existence. But I knew I had to attempt to find him in order to understand myself; I had to get close to him so that I could speak with him directly, ask him his purpose, question him—confront him.

That was why I decided to study theology in Paris.

I **PUT DOWN THE REPORT AND TAKE A PHOTOGRAPH OF** George Harrison out of my handbag. It looks like we're approaching Bourges, and yet I have barely glanced at the preface.

My first attempts with the iPod failed, but finally I succeeded in making it work. I lean back in my seat for a while and listen to music—the good old Beatles who always cheer me up, *Abbey Road* in this instance. I find it hard to get used to this gadget, but Sister Marie Joseph has done her best to instruct me and has been very patient with me. She had long had it in for my Walkman, which was admittedly on its last legs, and probably one of the last—according to her *the* last—still in use. I had taken it to the mender's several times, and finally it gave up the ghost, so I had no other choice but to modernize.

I miss the feel of the cassettes, which remain in their boxes in my cell, and I'm hopeless with the touch screen. Sister Marie Joseph has shown me countless times how I must slide my finger over it, but I still manage to regularly make a mess of it. The other day, while I was listening to the Brandenburg Concertos, I accidentally tapped the screen, and suddenly Diana Ross started singing. Not that I don't enjoy listening to her song about solitude, only I'd like to have some control over the process.

The photograph is actually of me and George Harrison in the rose garden. I am reposing, seated on the grass with the dog in my lap. We are gazing into each other's eyes, and he is stretching his muzzle toward me, so earnest and adoring that I feel close to tears as I contemplate the image. I miss him already, and I can see him before me as Marie Joseph and I drove away in the Renault, forlorn and whimpering in the doorway, as if he knew I wasn't coming back anytime soon. I know that Marie Joseph will take good care of him while I'm away, but all the same it upsets me to leave him.

The report. Eighteen typewritten pages. I had great difficulty composing it, and despite my best efforts every word was a chore. I was still in Iceland at the time, and when I spoke to Cardinal Raffin over the telephone, he advised me to take my time, to weigh and assess the events from the proper distance, to consider the broader context, to take into account all points of view. Those were his words, as he warned me not to exceed myself, not to let my emotions run away with me.

I have seen mistakes being made, Sister Johanna Marie, he said. And it's not easy to retract something that's written in black and white; it sticks in the mind. There it takes root, refuses to go away, even when other words are added, words intended to set things straight. We mustn't forget that there is only one judge of the living and the dead. Only one.

I had finished the report before Father August Frans's demise. Hours before, to be precise, and then I had added the two-page postscript after I returned home to the convent in France. During my stay in Iceland, I had lived close to Landakot Church, in a small apartment on Ljósvallagata, which I shared with two visiting nuns from Germany. On the strip of lawn outside the house was a laburnum tree, which I imagined in summer must look lovely, but whose limbs were bare and unappealing then. From the desk in my bedroom I had contemplated the tree, and the gray cemetery across the street, as I sat listening to the silence, which before had been broken by my sporadic tapping on the typewriter—a deep, insinuating silence that, far from calming me, increased my unease.

This time I had held nothing back in my report. I had refused to allow the "broader context" to cloud my vision. Even though I knew it might all be in vain.

I was exhausted when I went to bed that night, and yet I couldn't sleep. I could sense the finished report on the desk next to me, see the words before me in the dark, hear the *tap tap* of the typewriter. I waited until the German nuns had gone to Lauds, then I got dressed and went to the kitchen to make tea.

It was never my intention to follow them. I left the house at eight, when I knew that they and the other worshippers would no longer be in the church, for I had a sudden overwhelming urge to speak to my God, to tell him my thoughts.

What if I hadn't gone? What if I would have just handed in my report later that morning, and said my good-byes? What if I had just stayed home?

I had slept badly. Maybe that was the explanation. Maybe things would have been different had I been more rested.

The train is racing along. It will arrive in less than an hour and still the report lies on the seat beside me, unread. I finger the photograph of me and George Harrison, while the Beatles sing about the weight we carry. In the background, I see one of my favorite roses, *Rosa gallica*. She is hardy, tolerates the cold, and thrives in all types of soil. Yet she mustn't be neglected, for underneath she is delicate and needs caring for after surviving the winter. Then it's as if she says to me: *See how good I've been, now you be good to me. I do my very best, and we enjoy the warm summer sun, without thinking about how fleeting it is, or that fall is just around the corner.*

HAVE A FEELING OF SLIGHT APPREHENSION AS THE TRAIN pulls into Gare d'Austerlitz. On the train, my mind was so taken up with thoughts of Iceland, the terrible events that took place there, that I am completely unprepared for my arrival in Paris and the memories I know await me here. I put the report and the iPod in my little suitcase and wheel it off the train and then along the platform.

The weather couldn't be more splendid, and the people making their way hurriedly through the station have an air of summer. A group of students is gathering at the entrance, and inevitably my attire arouses some interest. That's how it always is, wherever I go, more so lately, as there are now fewer of us. However, when I smile at them, rather than looking away they smile back, and I see only warmth in their eyes.

I had been planning to rent a locker for my luggage at the station, but I realize that would be foolish, because then I would be forced to come back here, and of course that would be out of my way, for the train to the airport leaves from Gare du Nord or Saint-Michel/Notre Dame. My flight is at eleven o'clock tonight, and I am thinking of catching a train no later than half past eight. I want to arrive at the airport in good time, and moreover I suffer from night blindness—a condition that is worsening with age and is particularly bad when I'm tired.

I feel more unsure of myself than I had expected. I already sensed it when Sister Marie Joseph and I were planning my day in Paris on the convent computer. We sat side by side, her fingers gliding over the keyboard. She pulled up a map of Paris and showed me all the metro stations, the easiest way to get from A to B. The computer managed to confuse me, and as I took notes, I felt old and useless, and I said as much. It's only Google Maps, she replied, as if that explained everything, yet I was none the wiser.

Despite having written down everything carefully and gone over my itinerary on the train, I am daunted by the thought of traipsing around the city on my own. With the exception of the underground system, the city can't have changed much since I lived here and therefore my worries seem silly. I pause outside the station and decide to change my plan: I will not take the metro to Sacré-Coeur, but instead walk to the Sorbonne and from there down to the Seine. It isn't too hot for a stroll, and the wisps of cloud drifting across the sky create occasional pockets of comfortable shade on the streets.

I quickly become accustomed to pulling my suitcase, which is light, and the sound it makes almost comforting. As soon as I enter Le Jardin des Plantes, I feel a further sense of harmony; it is remarkable that this should happen the moment I am near some greenery. As I have plenty of time, and for my own enjoyment, I take a detour via the Grandes Serres, where I stand beside the open doors and inhale the aroma of damp soil.

When I first arrived to take up my place at the Sorbonne, in the late summer of 1965, I came across Le Jardin des Plantes during my first week in Paris and instantly fell in love with it. I discovered it by accident, for I usually went straight from class to the

Sacré-Coeur guesthouse in Montmartre, where I was fortunate enough to find paid employment. The guesthouse is right next to the basilica and the convent and offers accommodations to those coming to take part in devotional exercises and to commune with the Savior. I worked three hours a day in exchange for which I was given lodgings—a room in the cellar, which I shared with a Belgian student named Isabelle Bonnet, an extremely pious young woman. Like me, she was studying theology at the Sorbonne but was in her final year. She kept to herself, and we had little in common, but nonetheless we got along well enough as roommates. We each did our own thing and neither bothered the other.

The first year went by in a flash. Besides going to lectures and studying, I occasionally had to work four or five hours a day at the guesthouse, especially on weekends. I don't think I came any closer to my creator during those two semesters, although I read an awful lot about him. On the other hand, I was too busy to torment myself with thoughts about my inclinations. In fact, I succeeded in silencing them so completely during my first year in Paris that I began to tell myself that I had most likely been going through a phase, that this episode had only been a part of growing up, the result of me being a late developer. I think I almost managed to convince myself that the danger had passed, and nothing that summer suggested otherwise. I got a job at a café in my village, accepting all available shifts, because I needed the money. My sister and I only went swimming once at the lakes near Monsieur Hellard's house, and, even though it had been less than a year since I spied on the old man and his partner through the trees, the excursion had no effect on me. There was no one in the garden that day, and as we cycled by I managed to think of something other than the owner.

I did well my first year in college, and that fall I returned to Paris feeling full of myself. I had always had a gift for languages, but it was only there that my talents were put properly to the test. I am not exaggerating when I say that I was as surprised as my teachers, when, after my first year, I was fluent in German and achieved the highest grade in Latin, despite stiff competition.

I felt I knew the ropes when I got back and was able to take both my studies and my job at the guesthouse in my stride. I had managed to become terribly organized, making lists of things I aimed to achieve that winter—the neighborhoods I was going to get to know, places I wanted to visit. They included concert halls, museums, cafés and inexpensive restaurants, bookshops, parks, and a random collection of sites in almost every arrondissement. I told myself that now that I had gotten past the most difficult stage at school, I should take the opportunity to broaden my horizons.

I am recalling those bygone days as I walk to my old college along Rue des Écoles. It is farther than I remembered, and I soon cross to the shady side of the street. Gradually, I slacken my pace, pausing for a moment, for so many thoughts assail me that I have a hard time keeping track of them all. I let go of the handle of my suitcase and move as close as I can to the wall, so as not to get in the way of other pedestrians. With my handkerchief I wipe away the beads of sweat on my brow.

I am busy conjuring an image of myself almost half a century ago, when I hear my phone go off in my handbag. I become slightly flustered, for I had forgotten about it completely. I find it eventually and manage to read Sister Marie Joseph's text after a couple of tries: *Have you arrived safely in Paris?* But I can't remember how to reply, and after a few failed attempts, I give up and put the phone back in my bag.

WHEN I RETURNED TO COLLEGE, I WAS GIVEN the same room at the guesthouse as the year before and chose to sleep in my old bed, even though the one that had been Isabelle's had space for a bedside table next to it and a chest of drawers by the footboard, and was closer to the radiator, which barely heated the whole room in winter. But I am a creature of habit, and moreover, I wouldn't have known what to tell my new roommate if she found out that I had changed beds and asked me why. At best it would have been awkward. And I didn't dislike my side of the room, even if it was more cramped; for a bedside table, I used the windowsill, which was deep, and reached as far as the bedhead, and my clothes fitted easily in the shared wardrobe.

Although my previous roommate had been perfectly amiable toward me, she had made no effort to give me the benefit of her experience or go out of her way to show me around. Not that I had expected this, but when I learned that my new roommate was Icelandic, and this was her first time in Paris, I felt duty bound to assist her. She wasn't due to arrive for several days, whereas I had arrived early, as I wanted to have time to get myself ready for the winter semester. Also, I expect I felt rather ashamed about having gotten to know Paris so little during my first year, and embarrassingly had been forced to embroider the truth when my sister, Madeleine, and my coworkers at the café insisted on hearing about my experiences in the big city. I wasn't about to let that happen again.

The morning of my new roommate's arrival, I went out into the tiny garden next to the guesthouse, picked some flowers, and put them in a vase on her bedside table. At a secondhand bookshop near the college, I picked up a guide to Paris, aimed at the curious, experienced traveler. Before leaving it next to the vase of flowers, I got lost in it myself for almost an hour. The book served to remind me just how little I had seen of the city.

Although I wasn't supposed to start work until the following week, I felt I had no choice but to help out at breakfast that morning, but as soon as it was over, I went to look out for the new girl. I was told she was due sometime before lunch but wasn't given an exact time. The house quieted down late morning, after the guests went off, and I stood outside on the sidewalk, as though expecting her at any moment. Later, I liked to think that I had intuited her arrival, but of course I was just imagining it.

As expected, she came from the direction of the Sacré-Coeur, struggling with her two suitcases, one of which was clearly terribly heavy. I half ran toward her, helping her on the final stretch, but it was only when we reached the door that I made sure it was her.

Halla? From Iceland?

Oui.

Had I fallen for her even before she arrived? Strange as it sounds, I started to wonder whether I hadn't been looking forward so much to her arrival that I was well on my way to being enamored of her before I even set eyes on her. I told myself that we learn to love our Savior simply by thinking about him. Indeed, the only image we have of him is born of the words in the scriptures, which we re-create in our minds, bringing out the best in us. That image is one of hope and love, of tolerance and forgiveness, beauty and temperance. It is the image we would like to have of ourselves.

This is what I told myself, for Halla appeared to me as a vision of joy, of beauty incarnate, as she staggered toward me with her suitcases, suppressing a giggle, as though amused at having packed too many things and at finding herself in this strange place. She was quick to acknowledge my help by saying "Oh, thanks" and giving me a dazzling smile that would have caused the most battle-hardened warrior to lay down his arms. "Thank you, thank you very much," as if I were doing her a favor.

From the beginning I realized that she was as carefree as I was conscientious, as fleet of foot as I was lumbering when life got complicated or difficult. She laughed about how long it took her to find the right words in French, and yet she was instantly fearless, despite the mistakes she knew she was making. She asked me to correct her, and not to go easy on her.

In exchange, I'll teach you Icelandic, she said and laughed.

She noticed the flowers when we entered the room.

Did you do that? Really? She gave me a fleeting embrace, instantly noticing that I had also given her the best part of the room.

No, you must have this side. I insist.

But I refused to give in, and soon afterward she went off to meet our supervisor. But before leaving, she had opened her suit-cases then snapped them shut again, muttering to herself: What was I thinking? I've brought far too many things.

I stood still after she left the room, gazing at the flowers on the table, the guidebook beside them, her suitcases on the floor. I stood still and puzzled over what was happening to me. Strangely, amid my confusion, all I felt was happiness.

THE CATHOLIC BISHOP IN ICELAND HAD RECEIVED A letter, which he had forwarded to Rome. This was in the late '80s, during the papacy of John Paul II, when it was customary for bishops to sort out any problems in the priesthood without troubling the Vatican. However, the bishop of Iceland had rather hastily requested assistance, possibly to avoid his responsibilities, but more likely because he was frightened of those named in the letter and felt incapable of confronting them. Naturally, he didn't say this, but it was obvious to me from our first meeting.

In his defense, he had been appointed directly by the Vatican not by the archbishopric of Europe. The letter ended up at the Secretariat of State, on the desk of a man who had a reputation for solving conflicts, for making uncomfortable issues go away.

Raffin hadn't yet been named cardinal. But he had done well for himself, progressed within the Catholic hierarchy and gained the trust of his superiors. He was both resourceful and prudent, his brain a repository for information.

I hadn't spoken to him for years, but clearly he had stored my name somewhere in his brain. I suspect that deep down I had always feared the day would arrive when he would dredge it up again. More so during the first few years, of course, and yet somehow I never managed to feel at peace and was always half expecting the past to catch up with me—inevitably in association with Father Raffin.

But I'm going to try not to think of him. Not right now, at least, as I stroll around the grounds of my old college, peeking into the library, recalling so many things I believed I had forgotten. Before setting out this morning, I made myself a sandwich, which I wrapped in a napkin and placed in a paper bag, with an apple and a few grapes. I realize I am feeling peckish so I sit down on a bench beneath a tall maple tree to rest my tired bones. The shade offers an oasis of calm and peacefulness, despite the endless stream of tourists passing by.

The sandwich tastes good, the apple is ripe and the grapes sweet. My thoughts drift to George Harrison as he stood at the back door, watching me spread butter on my bread, and I am amazed at how long ago that seems. Perhaps the journey has made me lose my sense of time, which is usually so good that I have no need for a watch. When Sister Marie Joseph first joined us, she would amuse herself by asking me to guess the time and was always astonished at how accurate I was, to within a minute or two. I confess that I gladly took part in the game, as I have always been rather proud of my talent.

But now I feel disoriented, and I rummage in my bag for my phone to see whether I've guessed right that it's nearly four o'clock—or ten minutes to, to be exact.

I feel unnecessarily upset when the phone tells me that it's two minutes past four. There is no reason to despair, and clearly this twelve-minute difference is neither here nor there. And yet, I have the sense that something is wrong, and the feeling of unease I have been experiencing these past few days resurfaces.

I have no desire to travel to Iceland. I just want to take the train back home, to see George Harrison and go out into the rose garden tomorrow morning. They are forecasting sunny weather all week. I checked before I left. Glorious sunshine. I want to go home.

But gradually I get a hold of myself. I listen to the birds chirping in the maple tree, and after a while I calm down. There is no turning back, the sun goes down and the sun comes up, and with it comes yesterday. What has been will be once more. What was buried must arise again. And sin is never forgotten, but rather it dwells in the soul, from where it quietly makes its mark.

The letter attached to the back of the report is missing. I didn't notice it when I glanced at it on the train, but I can see it now as I flick through it here on the bench. I remember stapling it to the report before I sent it to Raffin; it was brief, a few lines written in the first week of Advent in 1987. He had given me the letter before my departure for Iceland two months later, even though I had no real use for it once I had read it. And yet he had handed it to me almost ceremoniously, and it occurred to me then that he might be trying to foist the responsibility onto me.

The marks left by the staples are clear on the photocopy I am holding now, two black dots on the top left-hand corner, and yet the letter is nowhere to be found. Possibly someone forgot to photocopy it alongside the report, or it has been lost over the years. But I doubt it; Cardinal Raffin leaves nothing to chance, and although I see no reason why he should wish to conceal the letter, as always when he is involved, I have my suspicions.

The letter wasn't signed. And Raffin had said, in so many words, that by forwarding it rather than dealing with the matter himself, the bishop had shied away from his obligations.

An American, he said, as if that explained everything, by the name of Andrew Johnson. A Jesuit.

I had no choice at that time but to do his bidding and travel to Iceland. Although he had previously reminded me of—and collected on—my indebtedness to him, and twenty years had gone by since he made his discovery known to me and explained the decision he faced, deep down I had always known that I would hear from him again. Indeed, when he showed me the letter in 1987, he spoke as if he had done me an enormous favor by keeping quiet, putting himself at risk when the correct thing would have been to report me. I had listened in silence, for I could think of nothing to say.

I put the report back in my suitcase, as I had better get a move on. From here I'll walk down to the Seine and over the bridge, and up the hill to the Sacré-Coeur. But I hesitate. So many things are best relegated to memory, so many steps best retraced only in the mind. Besides, it's quite a walk, and although I feel in fine fettle, I'm wondering whether taking the metro or even a taxi may be a better idea.

But that would be to give up, and after a while I set off along those same paths I trod as a young woman. I remember how excited I used to feel sometimes, hurrying home after my lectures, how I looked forward to seeing her. Sometimes I couldn't think of anything else and had a hard time concentrating on my studies. Not that we had anything planned, simply the daily routine: supper in the dining room, prayers, and an occasional stroll around the neighborhood. Just being in each other's company.

As I set off, I can see her before me, as so often through the years, sitting at the dining room table in our favorite spot, facing the doors. I see her turn to me and smile as I walk in. I have just gotten out of my last lecture, and I know she has been on the lookout for me.

Was she able to sense what I felt inside? I've reflected on this so often over the years, yet I still do not know the answer.

Perhaps during this trip, I may finally find out.

G**EORGE HARRISON PRICKS UP HIS EARS WHEN HE** hears his namesake sing about the sun. He seems to enjoy the same songs as I do, the slow ones particularly but livelier ones as well. He wags his tail and gazes up at me, as if to remind me how much we have in common, how fond we are of each other. Not simply how fond he is of me, but also to make clear that he knows how fond I am of him. That is what his gaze conveys to me, and his wagging tail.

It was Halla who introduced me to the Beatles. Of course, I'd heard the song about "Michelle," which had been popular in France— *Michelle, ma belle, sont des mots qui vont très bien ensemble, très bien ensemble . . .* —but that was the extent of my knowledge of the group. She seemed surprised to find the album *Revolver* in one of her suitcases, and she held the cover briefly before handing it to me.

I don't remember taking it with me. But they're so much fun, she said.

Her unpacking was as chaotic as her packing had clearly been. She had difficulty emptying her suitcases, and it took her several days to put away her things in the shared wardrobe or the chest of drawers at the foot of her bed. With each fresh item of cloth-ing she extracted, she gave a look of surprise and an occasional sigh, as though deciding whether to put it in the drawer or the wardrobe was a challenge. And yet in other ways she seemed so uncomplicated, so content with everything and everyone, happy and smiling, carefree.

In the end, I offered to help. She accepted gratefully, and we emptied the suitcases in two stages. We could have done it all at once, but as soon as the first suitcase was unpacked Halla felt the need to celebrate, and so we went to a café in the neighborhood, sat outside in the warm weather, and rewarded ourselves with straw-berries and ice cream.

During the first few days, I showed her Paris's most notewor-thy attractions and helped her to find her way around the city. She had a good sense of direction and a memory like a sponge but was also easily impressed and could spend ages contemplating a statue or a church. Although she found the Jardin du Luxembourg and the Hôtel des Invalides particularly impressive, she was even more enchanted with ordinary city streets, especially in the Latin Quar-ter, the houses with their pretty curtains or flowerpots by the en-trances, often remarking on how cozy and welcoming they were. She enjoyed looking at shop windows, not because she wished to buy anything, but rather to admire an imaginative display of col-ors and materials or simply to contemplate some minor decoration which would have escaped my notice had she not pointed it out.

Look at the dried lavender next to the skirt, she would say. And the faded photograph behind the bar of soap . . .

She spoke fondly of Reykjavík, although from her descriptions it sounded rather austere, without much in the way of beauty to hearten the discerning aesthete. Many of the local vegetables were alien to her, and she only knew the most common fruit. She asked lots of questions and was quick to retain the names of things, although naturally she sometimes got them mixed up. She soon solved that problem by keeping a journal, which she would read over in the evenings, before we went to bed, tired after carrying out our tasks at the guesthouse or from our sightseeing trips about town.

The weather was warm these days, occasionally hot. But soon the school year started, and before we knew it autumn had arrived. The leaves changed color, the nights grew chilly, and the wet weather came. Soon, we were both inundated with work, Halla even more so than I, as she had signed up for many classes, not just French language, but also French history and literature, art history, and math. We had in common that we were both conscientious, and at first she worried that she had taken on too much and would therefore be studying all the time. A small reading room up on the second floor offered some privacy, as few people used it, despite the wide range of books on theology and a wonderful view over the garden. We would often stay there until evening, and sometimes I would sit longer than necessary just to be with her. I did my best to help her out with her French, and if she got stuck she wouldn't hesitate to ask, as I had encouraged her to do.

In exchange I'll teach you Icelandic, she said more than once, and seemed genuinely surprised when I took her up on the offer.

Are you sure? she said.

Absolutely, I replied. I've always been very interested in languages.

The next day, my daily Icelandic lessons began, and I took them no less seriously than I did my theology lectures.

I must confess that I feared she would distance herself from me once her lectures started. I assumed she would make new friends among her fellow classmates, other foreigners who were also new to Paris; they would inevitably form a bond. And so, I wasn't surprised when the evening after school started, she met up with a group of other international students and found them worth telling me about—young men from Brazil and Japan, a girl from the States, a Danish woman in her thirties who had separated from her husband and was in search of a new life. I expected it would be like this most evenings, that I would see her only fleetingly, possibly no more than I had seen Isabelle the year before.

I was worried, yet I didn't discourage her. Not once. Neither directly nor indirectly. I don't say that to flatter myself, for naturally I had mixed feelings. More than anything, I wanted her to thrive and be happy, but at the same time I was terrified of my feelings and felt I had to rein them in and, hopefully, suppress them. That's what I tried to do, but obviously I failed, and on those evenings when she met up with her friends, I would anxiously wait for her to come home.

They turned out to be fewer than I had expected. She was a homebody by nature, and soon she was so busy with her coursework that most of her evenings were given over to study. She was content to meet her classmates during the day; sometimes they would have lunch together or go to a café, and she would tell me amusing stories about them when she got home, especially the Danish woman, who was taking full advantage of her newfound freedom.

To reward ourselves for completing an essay or finishing our homework, we would listen to the Beatles. There was a record player in the reading room and a small number of LPs on the shelf below, mostly sacred music, but also some classical records, mainly Bach if I remember correctly. We felt quite daring sneaking in there with *Revolver* and kept the sound turned down. Halla's favorites were "Yellow Submarine" and "Eleanor Rigby," but it was George Harrison who beguiled me from the very first. We amused ourselves by translating the lyrics into French, and this helped Halla make great strides with the language. *Mais si je semble agir méchant, il est seulement moi, ce n'ai pas mon esprit . . .*

As I reach the Seine, my phone beeps once more in my bag. *Marie Joseph*, I say to myself as I rummage for it and resolve to do better at responding to her this time around.

I HADN'T REALIZED HOW SHORT THE DAYS WERE NOR HOW black the darkness. Christmas 1987 had come and gone, and yet on the road from the airport a few weeks later I could still see decorations adorning some of the balconies and trees and, in the middle of a field on the outskirts of Reykjavík, the remains of a New Year's Eve bonfire. The bishop's young assistant met me at the central bus station, hurrying over to greet me the instant he spotted me.

Sister Johanna Marie? he said. And then, before I could reply, he added: As if there were any need to ask.

He was a cheerful, friendly young man, as was clear from his greeting, and showed none of the timidity or awkwardness that the nun's attire elicits in so many, especially the black habit worn by many orders, including mine. The young man took my suitcase, motioning toward a blue Toyota as he introduced himself: Páll Pétursson.

Good heavens, I replied, deciding at once to adopt the same relaxed attitude as he, two of our blessed apostles in one name, Paul and Peter.

It is remarkable how first encounters determine the way a relationship will develop. Our brief exchange at the bus station laid the foundation for Páll's and my friendship during my entire stay in Iceland. Those few words together with the short ride along Lake Tjörnin, through the center of town and up to Ljósvallagata, my questions about the music that filled the car when he turned it on. He looked a little embarrassed at having forgotten to turn off the stereo system when he parked, but his awkwardness evaporated when I asked him what the group was called. I don't remember the name, but he told me they were ex–migrant workers singing about cod, their days in fish factories—and capitalist exploitation.

Are you a revolutionary? I asked, and then, worried that I might have offended him, I added, the church could probably do with a few.

He smiled, and then suddenly it was as if he had resolved to get something off his chest.

I'm a Catholic, but only because of my parents. They are Catholic. I'm not very religious. I just needed a job after graduating from college with a degree in philosophy.

He parked outside the house on Ljósvallagata and carried my suitcase up the stairs. The German nuns greeted me, and while they weren't exactly talkative, they instructed me on how to use the washing machine in the basement, presented me with a set of keys to the main entrance and the door to our apartment, told me where the nearest grocery store was, and provided me with other bits of useful information. I was exhausted, and retired to my room early, but before going to bed I read the letter to the bishop once more.

I had it with me when I met Andrew Johnson the next morning, after Matins. He was younger than I expected, in his early forties, and it didn't take me long to see why he had sent the letter on, rather than deal with the issue himself. Although calm and courteous, he was clearly someone who disliked confrontation. I do not mean this as a criticism, for I too am averse to any sort of discord. But we cannot only do the things we like, as my mother used to say, and I considered that by taking on the post of bishop it was his duty to attend to all aspects of the job, not merely the less onerous ones.

We sat in his office, which was only a stone's throw from the church. It was nine in the morning, and still pitch-black outside. He hadn't drawn back the heavy curtains, and they made it seem darker still. He asked if I would like some tea. He seemed nervous.

I've not been here long, he said. Only a few months. It takes time to get used to everything here.

He is already excusing his lack of resolve, I thought, even as I nodded.

Many changes occurred during the time of my predecessor, Bishop Eijk. He died suddenly, blessed be his memory. I am the first Jesuit. Eijk belonged to the Montfortian order, as did those before him. And yet he had little in common with them, I have discovered. He had no more contact with his priests than was strictly necessary. Naturally, I am only just beginning to understand how things were done here, how everything works. This is a strange country.

He spoke rapidly, as though eager to impress upon me that the matters discussed in the letter had nothing to do with him, that he was unconnected to events in the past, and possibly even in the present.

I took out the letter, as well as the report Raffin had given me about the Catholic Church's activities in Iceland. Naturally, it offered a glossy image, but also contained some interesting material—information about the country's history, its people, important events.

I browsed through it while he waited uneasily.

According to this, your predecessor accomplished quite a bit, I said. It says here that he obtained funds for the diocese, chiefly from Germany, that he oversaw the renovation of the cathedral, instituted the decisions of the second Vatican parliament . . .

This is true, the bishop replied, and yet he had little contact with his priests, and none whatsoever with the school. It hasn't been easy for me to change that situation. It all takes time. —More tea?

He didn't wait for me to reply but rose to his feet and pressed a buzzer on his desk. Moments later, a middle-aged woman, who I assumed was his secretary, entered and took away the empty pot. I hadn't noticed her when I arrived.

He pulled aside the curtain enough to peek out then let it fall back into place, before sitting down again.

It gets light here so late, he said. I am finding it hard to get used to. The cold is a different matter, I am used to that, but I find the darkness oppressive.

I put down the report and handed him the letter. He hesitated before taking it. I couldn't blame him. I myself felt slightly unclean each time I read it.

He glanced at it.

Have you discussed the matter with those concerned? I asked.

No.

So they know nothing about the letter?

No, I sent it straight to Rome. I have no experience in such matters . . .

Have you any idea who sent it?

He shook his head.

And whoever it was hasn't contacted you further?

No.

Do you believe there is any foundation to these accusations?

I don't want to believe it.

His secretary knocked softly on the door before entering. She was carrying a fresh pot of tea and a plate of biscuits, which she set down on the table between us.

Nothing has aroused your suspicions? I continued after she left the room.

No, but I have no control over the school, I have barely set foot in the place. It is entirely Father August Frans's domain.

Does he try to keep you away?

He reflected for a moment.

Father August Frans has run the school since 1962. As far as I understand, he has enjoyed little support from the church and has kept the place going through his own efforts. Therefore, it is perhaps understandable that he doesn't welcome the involvement of a newly arrived bishop who is only just settling in.

What about Miss Stein?

I don't know much about her.

So you're not aware of anything that supports these allegations? No rumors, not a whisper?

No.

He handed me back the letter.

I felt I had no other choice but to take this to my superiors, he said. As I've already said, I have neither the knowledge nor the experience to deal with the matter. Although, naturally, I shall assist you in any way I can. As will Páll Pétursson, should you need him.

I couldn't help smiling when I heard his name. This didn't escape the bishop's notice.

He met you yesterday at the bus station, didn't he?

Yes, I said. He was most helpful.

Good, he said, good.

I'd be obliged if you would speak to Father August Frans to let him know I shall be in touch with him.

I saw his face cloud over.

What am I to say to him?

Just that I need to speak to him about a matter concerning the school.

He seemed relieved, and yet it was obvious that he dreaded the conversation.

Then you will start by interviewing him?

No, I said. I shall start with the two boys named in the letter. Or, more precisely, with their parents. Do you know them at all?

I've met the parents of one of the boys. They are active in the church. However, I've been here such a short time that I can't say I really know them.

Would Páll be able to put me in touch with them?

Yes, I think so, he said. But don't take him with you when you meet Father August Frans. He dislikes Páll. He says he's an unbeliever and that he does me no credit.

That's strange, I said. Páll and I spoke at length about the power of prayer, when he came to fetch me yesterday. He strikes me as a charming young man.

About the power of prayer, indeed? he said. I'm pleased to hear that.

It was ten o'clock when I left, and still dark outside. Perhaps I was imagining it, but it seemed colder, and the north wind that was sweeping the snow across the grass seeped all the way into my bones.

PÁLL PÉTURSSON PICKED ME UP AT LJÓSVALLAGATA the day after my meeting with the bishop. He had the names and address of both boys' parents.

I asked Hildur to find them for me, he said. The bishop's secretary, he added by way of explanation. She has worked at the bishop's office for over twenty years and knows everything and everyone. It wouldn't have been productive for me to contact the school.

I intimated that I wasn't surprised.

While I remember, I said, we spoke about the power of prayer when you picked me up from the bus station.

The power of prayer?

Yes. And we shall continue our conversation. Should the bishop ask . . .

He grinned.

One of the boys named in the letter, Jón Karlsson, lived on Vesturgata. Páll fetched the telephone directory, which he opened on the kitchen table, and showed me the street on the map at the back.

It's not far from here, I said. Can't we walk?

It's cold, he said, and the plows have left piles of snow on most of the sidewalks. I've got the car right outside.

In the blue Toyota, revolutionary rock music had been replaced by the mellow patter of the state radio announcer.

What year is the car? I asked.

He looked at me.

You're interested in cars?

A little, I said.

Eighty-two. It belongs to the church, but I have the use of it. My friends call it Jesus, he blurted, then instantly seemed to wish he hadn't.

Well, it is a reliable vehicle, I said, unassuming, economical, and it seldom breaks down.

He laughed, and suddenly I thought to myself: *What if I'd had children? A son, for example. He could have been Páll's age, and not unlike him, I would have hoped.*

Why does Father August Frans have a grudge against you?

I attended Landakot in first grade. My mother and father had wanted to send me to the school, even though at the time we lived in the Laugarnes neighborhood which is quite far. I didn't like it there, and they let me leave after a year. I don't think he's ever forgiven me for that.

We had reached the center of town.

I took the long way around, he said, pointing out the window: Austurvöllur Square, the parliament, Reykjavík Cathedral. Hotel Borg. But we can take a better look later.

Who is that? The statue?

That's Jón Sigurðsson. President Jón, as we call him.

He told me in more detail about the champion of the national independence movement, as he drove toward the port. That's the main pharmacy, Reykjavíkur Apótek, he said, and the old post office building.

Why didn't you like it?

What?

The school.

I always felt nervous, he said. It was terribly strict. And if you did something wrong, the punishments were quite harsh. I also missed my friends. They all went to the local school.

I decided not to press him further.

We came to a halt on Vesturgata, outside a small house clad with corrugated iron. A mound of snow blocked the pavement, and, unlike outside the neighbors' houses, it looked as if no attempt had been made to clear a path up to the front door.

I'm not sure where I can park, he said, as though thinking aloud. He drove farther on and finally found a place outside a shop set back from the road.

What do you know about the parents? I asked, before we stepped out of the car.

He felt in his jacket and pulled out a piece of paper, which he had scribbled on.

The mother's name is Karólína Símonardóttir, she's single. The father, Karl, was an American soldier at the NATO airbase in Keflavík.

Dead?

No, he left the country. It seems it was a brief liaison, he added, then fell silent.

He switched off the engine and cleared his throat softly.

What is this all about?

I asked him what the bishop had told him.

Nothing.

That didn't surprise me. I rummaged in my bag for the letter and handed it to him. He read it slowly then looked at me.

Is this true?

That's what we're trying to find out.

He stared straight ahead and didn't move. I took the letter out of his hands and put it back in my bag.

Let's see if she's at home, I said, opening the car door.

Why you? he asked.

Because I speak the language, I said, and quickly got out of the car.

SHOULDN'T HAVE REPLIED TO SISTER MARIE JOSEPH. But the text message she left really gave me no choice. *Is everything all right? Have you arrived safe and sound in Paris?* Of course, she was worrying unnecessarily, but I had undoubtedly made things worse by not responding sooner. I paused, managing this time to concentrate on the phone, to press the correct icon on the screen, and to make the keyboard appear. I typed in my reply (*yes, the journey went well, I have been killing time in the city*) and made the mistake of asking her about George Harrison.

I imagined him dozing as he always does at this time of day, lying in the shade next to the kitchen door, one eye open, or at least half open, waiting for the sun to sink in the sky, for the evening breeze that rustled the leaves, before getting up to take a stroll around his kingdom.

I hadn't expected her to reply straightaway, had put the phone back in my bag, and was setting off toward the Pont Neuf when it emitted that noise which I find so unpleasant. Marie Joseph says it can be changed, and I wish I'd asked her to see to that before I left, because it gives me a start whenever I hear it.

I halted, took out the phone again, and read the words that have been plaguing me for the past hour: *He keeps searching for you.*

I shouldn't have let it affect me, but now I feel completely out of sorts. I was on the verge of calling her but thought better of it. Instead I texted to tell her to give him the scraps of meat I put aside for him in the fridge and assured her he would soon get over it. Obviously, first and foremost I was trying to put my own mind at rest, and I thought I'd succeeded until she replied thirty seconds later to tell me he had lost his appetite. She is as quick at texting as I am slow, and there I stood motionless on the bridge, clutching my phone, all at once weak and anxious, and frankly in a terrible state.

I reasoned with myself, reminded myself that Sister Marie Joseph is inclined to exaggerate, that I'd been away less than one day, and that George Harrison couldn't possibly be this upset so soon. However, my arguments evaporated when I remembered the few times I've had to leave him for two or three hours, how anxious he had become, whimpering and whining, and only cheering up when I reappeared to the point where I have started to take him with me when I run my errands. When we are alone, he sits beside me on the passenger seat in the Renault and pokes his nose out the window, for he likes to feel the breeze, especially in hot weather. In fact, it was Sister Marie Agnès who suggested I should try not to leave him behind and was quite candid about how much his whining grates on her nerves when I am away. That was last year, after he chased the car and then disappeared. He was found hours later, wandering along the roadside, shaking all over, for he's not very courageous, the silly thing.

I wouldn't go as far as to say that I suffered the way George Harrison does where Halla was concerned, but I won't hide the fact that I never felt better than when I was in her presence, and I missed her when we were apart. I suspect the feeling was mutual, although I never deluded myself that she was the same way inclined as I, and I never crossed the line. It pains me to use the word to describe my behavior, and yet I suppose it's inevitable.

My love was reciprocated with friendship and affection, for which I was grateful—to God no less than to Halla, perhaps, or so I told him in my prayers, promising him to do whatever he wanted if only he did not take her from me.

I invited her home with me for Christmas so that she wouldn't be left in Paris on her own over the holidays. It snowed, and we went tobogganing, had snow fights, and went into town with my sister, Madeleine. It is pretty there at Christmas, the streets festive, the shop windows wreathed in decorations, and from morning to night the air is filled with the aroma of cooking coming from the restaurants. The square is crowded with people merrymaking, and outside the church the Christmas market is teeming, while beautiful music drifts from within. I enjoyed showing her around, introducing her to my friends and relatives, and succeeded, dare I say, in not allowing my feelings for her to be obvious to anyone. Madeleine did remark once that I needn't dote on her quite so much, but that was all she said, and from then on I reined myself in slightly, but not so much that anyone would have noticed.

She charmed everyone who met her, and my mother told me how lucky I was to have her as a roommate. The two of us were alone in the kitchen preparing breakfast when she said that, out of the blue, her back to me.

Yes, she's great, I replied simply.

Her words echoed in my head for a long time, as I tried to work out whether I could decipher something in her tone, but I never got to the bottom of it. Sometimes I convinced myself that this was her way of telling me she knew about my secret, at other times I told myself that she had been warning me, or even inviting me to open up to her.

I never puzzled so much over anything she said before or after. I often thought back to that morning in the kitchen and wondered what would have happened if Madeleine hadn't come through the back door just as Mother uttered those words. Would she have turned toward me, possibly in silence, and looked at me in such a way that I would understand what she was thinking? Would I have been able to conceal the truth from her then?

I thought about it often, I say using the past tense, but of course I still do. And I regret not having been honest with her, even though I have difficulty finding the right moment to have done so in my memory. I still don't know how she would have reacted.

I should have let things lie instead of sending Sister Marie Joseph a text message, but I couldn't help myself. Three text messages, to be precise, one every quarter of an hour, to ask whether George Harrison wasn't cheering up. *No*, she replied, *he has stopped searching for you, but he's still whining, and he refuses to eat.* Truth must be treated with care, and I would have been grateful to Sister Marie Joseph if she had been a little more economical with it.

But now the phone is back in my bag, and I am determined not to look at it again. My progress is slow: I have only just entered Rue Montorgueil. The clouds are dispersing as it gets hotter. I pause to wipe the beads of sweat off my brow, but I resist opening my bag. Admittedly, I gaze at it for a moment, but I resist, and, after a brief rest, I continue on my way.

PÁLL CLAMBERED OVER THE PILE OF SNOW ON THE sidewalk and knocked on the door. We had been forced to walk on the street from the car park, and I was still standing there in a deep wheel rut. Fortunately, there was hardly any traffic, but still it wasn't an ideal position. Páll was more concerned than I and glanced up and down the road continuously, as he waited for someone to come to the door. I could see no lights in the house, as I contemplated the threadbare curtains and a pair of blue porcelain figures on the windowsill. There was also an empty jar, and next to it a duster. The glass was misted up. The house looked run-down.

Only after the third knock did we hear footsteps and the door opened a crack. It was gloomy inside, but then a pale face appeared in the doorway. The woman peered out, apparently having difficulty adjusting to the dull morning light.

Karólína?

Yes, she replied, cautiously, as though unsure about confirming her name.

Páll introduced himself, then me, stepping aside so that she could see me out on the road. He asked if we could come in.

You've come at a bad moment, she said, then added, tentatively: Is this about my Jón?

Yes, said Páll.

Isn't he at school? He's always on time.

Before Páll could answer, she vanished from the doorway. But she quickly came back to tell us that, as she had thought, the boy wasn't in his room. With this, she clearly hoped we'd be on our way.

I admired Páll's powers of persuasion, his cordiality, for he finally managed to convince the woman to invite us in, assuring her that we wouldn't stay long, that we only wanted a few words with her about her son, who wasn't in any trouble, on the contrary.

He helped me over the mound of snow, and together we followed her into a small living room, where she switched on a lamp before motioning to us to take a seat on the sofa. She was in her dressing gown, which she held tight to her body as if guarding against a possible threat, but at last sat down facing us.

The house smelled of mold and stale cigarette smoke. On the table in front of us was an ashtray filled with stubs and a few out-of-date fashion magazines. I instantly noticed two framed photographs of a solider in uniform, one on the sideboard next to the window, the other on the piano at the far end of the living room. She saw me looking at the piano and said by way of explanation:

I'm a singer.

Páll smiled and told her that he had always been interested in music, then went straight to the point. We were speaking with parents of children at the school to ask about their experiences, because the church wanted to ensure that everyone was happy, and to make any improvements that were deemed necessary.

Jón is very happy, she broke in.

Good. And has that always been the case?

He has stopped misbehaving. It was just last year. He's stopped all that now.

She looked at me.

He's even started to say his prayers.

Does he have many friends? I asked.

The woman seemed surprised when I spoke Icelandic, and, perhaps because she had difficulty understanding my accent, she said:

What?

I repeated the question.

He spends most of the time alone nowadays, she said. They egged each other on, those boys. Baldur and Kári were a bad influence on him. He keeps to himself now.

Are they his classmates? I asked

No, she said, sitting up straight in her seat. They aren't good students like him. They go to the school on Öldugata.

Does he like his teachers? I asked.

Yes.

And the headmaster?

She looked at Páll, as if he might know the answer, and then at me.

Yes.

Have you gotten to know Father August Frans yourself? I asked.

Yes, and we're very grateful to him.

She fidgeted once more in her seat.

I need to rest. Is there anything else?

I shook my head.

Don't hesitate to be in touch if you think of anything else, said Páll.

We got up and went out to the front door where we'd left our shoes. A small puddle had formed around them.

Forgive my lack of hospitality, she said, but I'm not feeling very well.

We wished her a speedy recovery and apologized for bothering her.

As soon as Páll grasped the handle and opened the door, she said in a hushed voice: So you'll tell Father August Frans that everything is okay, won't you?

Páll was about to explain that we weren't there on behalf of the priest, but glanced at me and stopped short. Instead, he simply nodded.

It's not easy raising a lively young lad on your own, she said. His father is away a lot. Father August Frans has been a great help to us.

We clambered over the snowdrift and followed the tire tracks back to the small parking lot. It had only just gotten light, yet I had the impression it was already getting dark again. A bank of gray clouds hung over the bay.

He went out that way, said Páll, pointing to the footprints in the snow, leading away from the back door of the house.

We paused for a moment, tracing the footprints that crossed the road in front of us and continued toward the school.

When we climbed back into the car, I could still smell the stale cigarette smoke.

T HE OTHER BOY, KRISTJÁN HERMANNSSON, LIVED UP
on Bergstaðastræti, on the first floor of a two-story stone
house set back from the road. We drove the long way
around from Vesturgata, via the old harbor, and from
there to the shipyard, where we stopped on the quayside and
looked out over the sound. It had started to snow.

I sensed that Páll was uneasy, although he had managed to
hide it rather well at Karólína's house. Clearly, I shouldn't have involved him in the affair without preparing him first, and I blamed
myself for not having thought things through properly. For my
part, I'd had no choice in the matter, but that didn't apply to him.
I ought to have explained to him the nature of my mission before
asking him to accompany me.

I said as much while we sat in the car on the quayside.

It was wrong of me not to warn you, I said. And I apologize.
You needn't be part of this.

He said nothing. A small fishing boat was casting off, and I
watched the cone of light sweeping before it, as it disappeared into
the flurry of snow.

Who do you think sent the letter? he said at last.

I've no idea. But whoever wrote it is an insider.

A teacher?

Possibly. Or a parent. Who knows?

He fell silent, stared out the window, then quietly shook his hand.

Can this really be true?

I don't know whether he was expecting a response or perhaps some thoughts about guilt and innocence, or a sober reflection about the difficulties we faced, previous experiences that might offer clues, insights into the nature of man—firm guidance.

I felt like telling him the truth: that I was no Sherlock Holmes, and that my experience proved only that I was ineffectual, which was doubtless why Cardinal Raffin had sent me here. Not because of my knowledge of Icelandic, as he had suggested, but rather because of his belief that I would achieve nothing. Judging from past experience, he had every reason to count on my inability.

As we sat looking out over the sound, I wish I could claim now that I suddenly decided to defy Raffin, to show him what I was capable of, promising to leave no stone unturned until everything was revealed. But the truth was that, as I watched the wipers sweep the snow off the windscreen, all I could think of was how to tie up the investigation, if one could call it that, as soon as possible.

May I see the letter again?

I reached into my bag and handed it to him.

Is this a man or a woman's handwriting? he said after contemplating it for a little while.

I had of course wondered about that myself, but hadn't reached any conclusion. I told him so.

He scratched his head.

The "L" and the "K" make me think it was written by a woman, he said, as does the "D." But not the "M" the "N" or the "T." I'm not sure about the other letters . . .

I hadn't examined the letters as closely as he had, but when I did, I thought he was right, save for the "T."

We're none the wiser, then, I said, realizing at once that it might sound as if I was expecting him to assist me, and so I added: But I think it's probably best you stay out of this.

I'm afraid you're stuck with me and Jesus, he responded, gently tapping the dashboard as he drove off down the quayside, making a U-turn at the widest point.

I felt relief and was about to thank him when he added:

Have you been involved in many cases like this?

I gave a start, but managed to reply.

One.

Can you tell me about it?

HOW LONG DID RAFFIN THINK IT WOULD BE BEFORE I went looking for Halla Hjartardóttir? Did he have a specific idea in mind—a day, or two, a week, a fortnight—or was he content in his belief that sooner or later I would fall prey to temptation? And yet, despite counting on my weaknesses, he also wanted to be on the safe side, and so before I left, he warned me not to let myself give in—on the pretext, naturally, that he was concerned about my welfare.

I am loath to ask you this, Sister Johanna, and I trust there is no need, however, I cannot help but mention . . .

I forget the exact wording of his question, but he succeeded in unsettling me, not least because, as he spoke, the image of Halla popped into my head. It felt as if he had been reading my mind, waiting for her to appear before hurling the question at me, fixing me with his gaze the whole time, as if he were in complete control of the conversation. He drew out our exchange, prolonged it unnecessarily, showing perfunctory signs of sympathy. He said he hoped he wasn't placing me in an awkward position, we didn't wish to awaken any old ghosts, and encouraged me to speak openly if I thought the trip might upset me; Reykjavík was a small town, where I might bump into her by chance. Then he said something about our Savior, about man's imperfections, that we all had our demons, that I had fought mine off with admirable resolve, and that the last thing he wanted was to be responsible for me losing that battle.

I should point out that he did this so tastefully that anyone observing could only have concluded that he had shown great sensitivity. However, I could read his thoughts as well as he could read mine, and so we sat there, half listening to each other's words, fully aware of the hidden messages they contained.

I am surprised that you have kept up your Icelandic all this time, he said.

Not only my Icelandic, I said, other languages too.

He smiled, and I kicked myself for taking the bait and going on the defensive.

Saint-Amand had been his parish when I came to the convent thirty years ago, having spent four years at a mission in Africa and prior to that almost as long at a convent in Jouarre. During those eight years, I hadn't had any dealings with Raffin, and while I naturally remembered him all too well, I had no idea what had become of him and, truth to tell, tried to think about him as little as possible. And so, it came as something of a shock to discover his involvement in my affairs, as he had clearly had a hand in me ending up in Saint-Amand-Montrond, as opposed to Ligueux in the south, or Valognes in Normandy, which had also been a possibility.

Father Raffin speaks highly of you, said Sister Marie Agnès, after I had been at the convent for about a month. He says you showed great inner strength in the face of a difficult dilemma . . .

She is inquisitive, almost nosy, by nature, and looked at me as though expecting me to enlighten her as to the nature of that dilemma, but I didn't trust myself to say anything about my time in Paris for fear of arousing suspicions, and so I changed the subject.

When Father Raffin visited the convent a few days later, he was quick to make it clear that he had been following my progress over the years. He asked about the time I had spent in Uganda, and in the Congo, he spoke of Jouarre's history, in particular of Charlotte de Bourbon, about whom I'd read much, and whom I admired, an attitude he probably did not share.

Judging from his manner, he seemed principally concerned with my welfare, feeling a duty of guardianship toward me. I cannot help admitting that he was so convincing that for a long time I felt confused, veering between doubt on the one hand and gratitude on the other, sometimes even reproaching myself for being churlish.

I felt relieved when a year later he was given a post at the Vatican. I was out when he came to say his farewells to Sister Marie Agnès, but she told me he had sent his regards. She was duly impressed.

I heard nothing from him until five years later when, out of the blue, he announced his arrival. I think I suspected immediately that it was me he wanted to see, although he didn't say so. That was three years before my trip to Iceland in 1988, the prologue to it, if I can call it that. Perhaps there was nothing I could have done. Perhaps I shouldn't blame myself.

"It's a small town," he had said, before handing me the letter, whose author Páll Pétursson and I would wonder about. "You might bump into her . . ."

I noticed the directory in the hallway my first morning at Ljós-vallagata. It was sitting innocently next to the black telephone and a small vase containing dried flowers. Even so, I contemplated it for a moment before going into the kitchen, where the German nuns were waiting for me. There we ate porridge and discussed the shortness of the days over coffee.

I didn't touch the telephone directory until the following evening. My German sisters had gone out, and I walked past it several times before picking it up and taking it with me into the living room. There I sat for a good while with it in my lap, struggling with doubt and temptation, until at last I gave up and began my search for Halla Hjartardóttir.

MY SOUL CLINGS TO THE DUST, GIVE ME LIFE according to your word . . .

I have always sought strength in the ritual of prayer, not merely in the words themselves, the psalms and verses, but in everything associated with it: the customs, most of which have remained unchanged for centuries, the constant repetition, the inherent rhythms, the closeness of the sisters when we sing in unison, my inner self in the silence—and of course God, in those instances when I feel his presence.

The words flow from me as from an actor who has been playing the same role for half a century. I rarely fumble or need to consult my prayer book to refresh my memory. Let me be clear that by using that analogy I do not wish to imply that I am putting on a show, although I confess that sometimes I do allow my thoughts to drift during prayers. But even then, I benefit from the calm they bring and am able to contemplate various matters that otherwise might put me on edge.

I attended Matins before Sister Marie Joseph drove me to the train station, but now it is almost five o'clock, and I feel a need for the peace and rest prayer brings. It occurred to me to make a detour and stop off at Saint-Eugène-Sainte-Cécile, but I decided that I was perfectly capable of waiting until I reach my destination.

My sojourn has taken longer than I had anticipated. Age is of course a factor, and yet for the past fifteen minutes or so, I feel as if I am purposely half dragging my heels. I could try to convince myself that this is due to fatigue and ignore the anxiety that has taken hold of me, but since I have promised to be sincere, that probably won't work. The truth is that I considered turning back the moment I crossed Rue Lamartine, for it is obvious to me that by visiting Sacré-Coeur I will not change the past, merely open up old wounds, breathe new life into memories that I have tried to push from my mind. That is why I pause again when I glimpse the hill between the houses at the far end of the street, the square at the foot of the hill, and the steps leading up to the Sacré-Coeur. I hesitate, look back over my shoulder, then I pull myself together, wipe the sweat from my brow, and continue on my way, slowly, of course.

In my suitcase are the books Halla gave me for Christmas. I need the bilingual dictionaries, both French-Icelandic and Icelandic-French, but I could have left the copy of *My First Reading Book* behind in my cell. Inside is the card that came with the gift—"Happy Christmas, dearest Pauline, I am sure your Icelandic will soon be better than my French . . ."

She had asked her parents to buy the dictionaries for her, but the copy of *My First Reading Book* was one she was given when she started learning how to read. Laughing, she apologized for the doodles which appeared on two of the pages, a yellow sun and a bird in a tree, explaining that her mother hadn't been too pleased with her artistic endeavors.

We had sat in the living room at my parents' house and opened our presents. It had been evening, the lengthy Christmas dinner over, and a fire was blazing in the hearth. I clutched *My First Reading Book* longer than I had intended, only setting it aside when I noticed my mother looking at me.

I take a long time mounting the steps. My suitcase isn't so heavy, even with the books which I should maybe have left at home, but I hadn't expected it to be quite so arduous, dragging it up the hill. I see the basilica before me, whiter than I remembered, as it stretches up into the bright blue heavens. I catch my breath and think about the peace awaiting me in the pews, the silence that will envelop me, the words waiting to quicken my lips.

Open my eyes, that I may behold wondrous things out of your law. I am a stranger in the earth: hide not your commandments from me.

Halfway up the steps, a young man turns to me to ask if I need help with my suitcase. He looks no older than twenty, as does the girl who is with him. They are obviously keen to help, but I ask if I am not right in thinking they are on their way down. Yes, they reply, quickly adding that they don't mind going up again.

I accept their offer, glad of the help, as well as the company. They don't seem in any hurry, and they tell me so, without making me feel like a lame old woman.

Every so often, the girl stops to glance over her shoulder at the view; of course I understand what she's up to, and I smile to myself. She reminds me of Sister Marie Joseph: whenever she worries that I'm working too hard in the garden, she comes over and starts to lend a hand, quite unnecessarily.

As we ascend the steps, we chat about this and that. They tell me they are both at college in Paris; he is Belgian and she is Parisian. He studies philosophy and she engineering. They share a love of traveling and music, and he tells me they are hoping to go to India next summer. She pulls a strange face when he announces this, and from her expression I gather they have yet to make a firm decision.

They seem in no hurry to leave once we reach the top, and the girl asks me if I am going to enter the church. I tell her that I am, that the fact is I feel the need to pray, that the journey has upset my routine.

We've just been inside, she says.

I wait.

We were praying . . . Well, I was, anyhow.

She looks at her boyfriend, who has a sheepish expression. Something is clearly bothering them, and for some reason, the girl has decided that it is all right for me to know about it.

Would you like to come inside with me? I ask.

The girl looks at him.

If you'd like us to.

He says this in a casual voice that betrays no resentment or impatience. He takes her hand, and I see him squeeze it with obvious affection.

I don't mind if you don't come in, she says to him, as we approach the entrance. Then she turns to me, adding by way of explanation: He's an atheist, you see, but I had a very religious upbringing. My parents don't know about our relationship.

I look at him, and something tells me he has misread my expression, for it is certainly not my intention to censure him at all. But he apologizes: Unfortunately, I can't pretend to believe in God when I don't.

He seems a little anxious, and I think to myself how strange it is to be seen as someone who possesses wisdom or authority by people I have never met before. It even occurs to me that they may not have approached me on the steps merely by chance. A far more likely explanation is that they simply took the opportunity once we were engaged in friendly conversation.

It is obvious how deeply they care for each other, how much he adores her, and how much the burden of their sin weighs upon her. They look back at me, as though expecting me to say something that will remove all their cares, wave a magic wand that joins together that which cannot be joined, turns black to white, drives the guilt from their hearts.

I am about to say that I cannot help them, that I have enough difficulty bearing my own cross, I am about to take my leave. But fortunately I stop myself, for it isn't every day that we can perform a good deed simply by speaking our mind.

Will it kill you to come with us into the church? I ask him.

My lighthearted tone takes him off guard, and for a moment he seems unsure what to make of me.

Yes, but I can't . . .

Are you capable of thinking about your girlfriend and about love for a few minutes?

Of course, but . . .

Then you will help him with the teachings of apostle Paul, I say to her.

She nods, and her smile is one of relief. Truth be told, I am surprised, because of course she must know Paul's First Epistle to the Corinthians by heart. Yet sometimes it takes a stranger to show people what is obvious, not in mirrors or riddles, but face-to-face.

Although the biblical reference clearly goes over the boy's head, he can see the change in his girlfriend. He looks at her, and she recites the closing words of the thirteenth verse to him—a sentence I repeated to myself so often when I was their age, to no avail.

And now these three remain, faith, hope and love. But the greatest of these is love.

He stands motionless for a moment, but then together we enter the cool interior of the church.

THEY'RE NOW SITTING BESIDE ME ON THE PEW, AND I imagine that they are thinking about Corinthians—and each other. I am holding my prayer book, which I retrieved from my suitcase before we sat down, but I haven't opened it yet. Sometimes I leave it unopened, yet I always like to hold it in my hands. I've had it since the first year I came to Paris.

I was eager to be inside this place of calm, and it's therefore disappointing that I'm having a hard time concentrating. It isn't the young couple that's distracting me, but my own mind, for rather than allow this silence to permeate my soul, I start to remember things I know will only trouble me. And not for the first time.

I start to think about when I first met Raffin. It was soon after Christmas; Halla and I were listening to the *Sgt. Pepper's* album, a gift from her brother. We were sitting on the floor in the reading room, ears pressed to the speakers, because we had to keep the volume low and didn't want to miss a single note. We were still only halfway through the A side, I seem to recall. I don't know how long he had been standing in the doorway before we noticed him, but I have never forgotten his expression. Beneath the apparent air of good-natured tolerance, he looked as if he had caught us red-handed.

They are popular with young people, he said, giving that sly smile of his, as if he felt superior not just to us, but to all young people, although as far as I could see he was only a few years older than us.

He introduced himself. Father Raffin, a new deacon at the Sacré-Coeur.

I removed the record from the turntable and slipped it back into its sleeve. He watched me in silence, remarking as I switched off the record player, "Not on my account."

I had collected myself and realized how foolish my response had been. And yet from that very first meeting, he gave off a feeling of menace that was belied by his physical presence. I got angry. How could I let him dictate to us?

We don't need your permission to listen to music in here, I heard myself say, as I brushed past him, Halla close behind. He was slightly taken aback, but quickly recovered his composure, and, as we stalked off somehow I sensed that sly smile playing on his lips once more.

Over the next weeks and months, I would see him around, but I kept my distance. I noticed him watching me, and when we did bump into each other, he would greet me politely. I responded in kind but was careful not to engage with him. On the other hand, I would listen attentively whenever I heard people talking about him. Apparently, he graduated from college with the highest grades and instantly attracted the attention of the church hierarchy. It was said that he had a future ahead of him.

Not long after our first encounter with him, Halla said to me: He asked about you.

Who?

The deacon. I ran into him yesterday when I was cleaning. He told me he hadn't intended to bother us. He all but apologized.

All but, I was about to say, but stopped myself.

He was quite friendly, she added.

I didn't really give the new deacon much thought. I had enough on my hands with all the college work and, on top of it, Halla deciding to sign us up for dance classes twice a week. I laughed when she first suggested it, but of course I went along with the idea. Not only was her enthusiasm catching, but I felt happiest when I was near her, no matter the occasion.

Following the incident in the reading room, Raffin took every opportunity to engage Halla in conversation. I didn't find out until later, but clearly his intention was to get to know her, not that she put it like that, for she didn't question his motives. Most days she finished school earlier than I, and Raffin seemed to lie in wait for her when she came home to have a snack in the kitchen, or when she was carrying out her chores at the guesthouse—cleaning and making the beds, tidying the sitting room. Then he would pop his head around the door and strike up a conversation with her, always in a casual, friendly manner. He would ask questions about Iceland, for example, which he had clearly acquainted himself with, or just about this and that, always taking care not to outstay his welcome.

And so she had no reason to be on her guard any more than when she spoke to other staff members, nuns, or guests. She treated everyone with the same natural warmth, gaiety, and lightheartedness, never for a moment suspecting that her interlocutors' motives might be anything but good and positive. However, Raffin was shrewd, and I do not blame her for anything.

In February, the weather grew cold, as one would have expected at that time of year, but then suddenly the temperature dropped to ten degrees below zero. The college was so chilly that we had to wear our coats and scarves to lectures, some people even kept their hats on. My hands are cold at the best of times, and I had to buy fingerless gloves so that I could take notes. I wasn't the only one. The banks of the Seine froze over, and people avoided staying outside, darted between buildings, traveled on buses or on the metro, piled into cafés to keep warm.

You must be used to this, people would say to Halla, who smiled benevolently, because of course she was as cold as everyone else.

In the evenings we would sit in the kitchen with the staff at the guesthouse, or in the reading room, because our bedroom was freezing, even Halla's side. But at night we had no choice, and despite wrapping up before we got into bed, it wasn't enough. The bedclothes were inadequate—in fact they were heavy blankets that offered little warmth—and the radiator gave off a meager heat.

It was she who asked if I wanted to climb in beside her. We had just turned out the lights and were shivering in our separate beds—especially me, as the radiator was on her side. It was a simple matter of expediency, on her part as much as mine; two covers were better than one, and with the heat of each other's bodies we soon warmed up.

I won't deny that I enjoyed lying next to her, listening to her breathing, feeling her body close to mine. We slept back to back, but that was enough for me, and I certainly had no improper thoughts. There we lay at night, enveloped in each other's warmth, while the city was gripped by cold and the moon hung frozen in the heavens, there we lay, and my only concern was that it would soon get warmer.

The cold snap lasted two weeks, and when it passed, I took the initiative and returned to my own bed, fearful of betraying my true feelings for her.

Oh, I'm going to miss you, she said, after we had turned out the light and said good night. Seconds later, she was asleep.

It isn't hard to imagine how Raffin came to know of our arrangement, and of course Halla had no idea of the consequences. But he had seen through me, he knew what she didn't know. And when confronted, I was helpless to try to hide it; I stood exposed, unable to speak, and of course that was enough for him.

I COULDN'T FIND HER IN THE DIRECTORY—EITHER IN REYK-
javík or in the rest of the country. I remember her telling me
that in Iceland people were listed under their first names, so
that wasn't a problem, and I soon realized that I had to include
in my search all the districts outside the capital, listed at the back.
But my search proved useless: according to the directory, nowhere
in Iceland was there a Halla Hjartardóttir; not in the Westfjords
or the Eastfjords, not up north, nowhere in the south.

I was seized by a sudden panic, and I opened the directory
again, renewing my search for Halla, as if my life depended on it.
Of course, I found nothing, although fortunately I started gradually to calm down, realizing how foolish my reaction had been.

The most likely explanation was that her husband's name was
registered in the directory instead of hers. It also dawned on me
that she might have moved abroad. For some reason, I began to
imagine her living in Madrid or Florence—as if those cities suited
her, those smiling eyes, those slim shoulders, her slender fingers as
she hooked her hair absent-mindedly behind her ear. Or in Paris,
and then my heart missed a beat. At last I caught hold of myself
and started to think rationally once more.

The last time I had heard from her was the autumn after she

moved back to Iceland. She was at the University of Iceland, study-ing French and history. She said she liked it there, but missed Paris, and me. A lot. She copied out some Beatles lyrics in her last letter, from track five of the B side of *Revolver*, if I remember correctly.

It was around that time that I made my final decision to be-come a nun and started my aspirancy at a tiny convent in the nineteenth arrondissement. I continued my studies at the Sor-bonne, where I added Icelandic as one of my subjects, and had an hour's tutoring a week with a Norwegian professor, who had difficulty concealing his atheism.

I took Halla's letters with me to the convent and kept them for years. No, that isn't quite right. It would be more accurate to say that I carried them around with me and thought about them every single day. But finally I threw them away, when I realized that I was using them to punish myself. Not to relive wonderful moments, or to find comfort in them, but rather to tear myself apart, to remind myself where I had gone wrong in life. And Halla deserved better than that—this couldn't be the epitaph to our re-lationship, so one autumn, long ago, when I first arrived at Saint-Amand-Montrond, I threw them on the bonfire out in the garden, together with the dead leaves and twigs.

I thought of her letters, as I put down the directory and went over to the living room window. It was not yet four but it was al-ready getting dark. The sky was overcast, and even the snow had turned a grayish hue and did little to brighten things up. I started to think about our visit to Bergstaðastræti the day before.

After leaving the harbor, Páll and I had decided to try our luck and see if Kristján Hermannsson's parents were home. We parked outside and approached the house up a narrow pathway of trodden snow, only to retrace our steps a minute later when no one came to the door. Later that evening, Páll got hold of the husband on the phone and told him we would be stopping by the following day. Obviously, the man wanted to know the reason for this visit, but Páll said he had feigned ignorance, playing down his own role, claiming he was merely assisting an emissary of the church, who wanted to meet him and his spouse.

The couple greeted us on the doorstep, he in a white shirt and red tie, she in a dress. The husband was tall and rather stocky, his wife the opposite. There was no hint of suspicion on their faces, or that they considered our visit unusual; on the contrary, they seemed happy to see us.

Welcome, he said, introducing himself. Hermann Atlason. And this is my wife, Jenný.

We all shook hands, and they ushered us into the living room, where coffee cups and side plates were laid out on the table. A picture of our Savior hung on the wall above the sofa where Páll and I sat down, and there was another of the pope between the windows facing the street. I had noticed a large but simple cross in the hallway.

It's a little chilly outside, Hermann said, after they had complimented me on my Icelandic. I had yet to discover how impressed Icelanders were by me speaking their language, and most conversations began by them asking me how I came to learn it, praising my vocabulary as well as my pronunciation, even though I had to repeat myself every now and then, and sometimes made mistakes, particularly with the inflections and irregular verbs. Occasionally, I would also let the prepositions confuse me for they are particularly tricky.

You need a cup of coffee to warm you up, don't you? he continued, and there's rhubarb pie, which my Jenný made this morning.

It's still warm, said the woman, as she disappeared quickly into the kitchen.

All of a sudden, I had the impression of traveling back thirty years in time. Not only did their home strike me as traditionalist, or possibly opposed to modernity, but the roles of husband and wife seemed to belong to my parents' generation. Hermann spoke for them both, while she listened. He was talkative, and I was only too happy for him to keep talking, if it meant he didn't ask about the reason for our visit; that way, I thought, I might be able to broach the subject discreetly, or at least draw some conclusions, shine some light on things, without having to be too straightforward.

He was an office manager at the state Treasury Department, she was a housewife. He talked about his job, the extravagances of the government, the lack of strict fiscal policies.

We do our best, but more often than not, we are overridden. Do you understand the expression overridden?

I nodded.

There is too much frivolousness in this country, he went on. In many areas. It is all down to a lack of discipline. I was brought up in the Catholic faith and learned rigor and diligence from an early age. I was taught what it means to be responsible to our Savior. My wife, Jenný, converted to the faith when we married, and we live according to its teachings to the best of our ability.

We Icelandic Catholics have to stick together, because there are so few of us. I'm not saying that people resent us, although they do consider us slightly strange. Halldór Laxness's conversion didn't improve matters, understandably, because he is a little different, shall we say. And, to be honest, in my opinion, he is too effusive about his faith. Most Icelanders don't know the difference between Catholicism and Protestantism. They really have no idea. Few are acquainted with the Ten Commandments, they are content to know the Lord's Prayer, to be baptized and confirmed, largely it would seem as an excuse to throw a party and receive gifts. They only ever hear the scriptures read at funerals, or if they happen to switch on the radio between eleven and twelve on a Sunday morning, because no one attends church anymore, except for old women who are close to death. I'm not exaggerating, am I, Jenný?

No, said Jenný, putting down the delicious-smelling pie on the table. You're not exaggerating.

And the coffee, is it ready?

Just coming, she said, hurrying to the kitchen and returning immediately to fill our cups.

What do you think of our new bishop? Hermann asked Páll, leaning back in his chair, as he bit into a piece of pie.

He's fine.

A Jesuit, said Hermann. And an American. Needless to say, that came as a bit of a shock. We haven't gotten to know him well yet, but we hope for the best. It can't be easy stepping into Bishop Eijk's shoes, blessed be his memory. And of course we've become accustomed to our bishops belonging to the Montfort order. That arrangement has been good for us. Fortunately, though, I haven't noticed any changes. You don't think he is planning to revolution-ize things, do you?

Páll said he thought it unlikely; the new bishop understood tradition and had great respect for the work carried out by his pre-decessor. I found it amusing how punctilious Páll could be.

I'm glad to hear that, said Hermann.

The pie was delicious, and I complimented Jenný. Páll agreed, and she told us she baked it regularly, adding that it was popular at parish meetings.

And it's healthy, too, said Hermann, oatmeal and rhubarb.

Now tell me about yourself, he went on, turning his attention to me. The blessed Sisters of Saint Joseph have done admirable work here over the decades. Jenný and I are delighted to be among the first to welcome you to Iceland.

I should have expected that they would assume I was one of the sisters, but I was caught off guard. I felt Páll stir uneasily on the sofa beside me. I reached for my napkin, wiped my mouth, and cleared my throat softly.

I am not strictly a member of the order of Saint Joseph, I said, although naturally I agree wholeheartedly that they have done a magnificent job, both here in Iceland and in the wider world. They are a shining example to us all. I am here on behalf of the Vatican to acquaint myself with the work of the parish, as well as the connection between the church and the school—and of course to brush up on my Icelandic, not before time.

They were clearly impressed by the mention of the Vatican, but I sensed at once that they were wondering what business I had with them. Believing that I had thus far avoided telling a lie, I decided to carry on, before they asked me something to which I would be unable to give an honest answer.

You do a great deal of work for the parish, I said, and your son is at the school, is he not?

Yes, our Kristján is in fifth grade, said Jenný, glancing toward the window, where a family photograph in a silver frame sat on a side table. Hermann rose to fetch it.

Our Kristján has learned a lot at the Catholic school, he said, handing me the picture. Discipline, self-control, and godliness.

I contemplated the photograph; it was taken by a professional, and the family were in their Sunday best. Kristján wore a tie, a white shirt, and a blue V-necked sweater. It looked recent.

He's a good-looking boy, I said. Does he like school?

I noticed Jený hesitate and look at her husband.

Yes, said Hermann, emphatically. He likes it very much.

He fell silent, and I had the impression he was waiting to see what I would say next.

What is his favorite subject? I asked.

Math, replied Jený. He's very good at arithmetic.

He likes school very much, Hermann repeated. Father August Frans has worked miracles, and, truth be told, without much support from the church. Jený and I are grateful to him, exceedingly grateful.

He glanced at his wife, who looked briefly down at her lap, before nodding in agreement.

Miracles, her husband repeated.

I don't doubt it, I said, wishing instantly that I had held my tongue, for something in my tone seemed to make him suspicious.

Have you not been to see him?

Not yet, but I intend to, I replied.

He looked straight at me. All of a sudden, his manner changed, from one of friendliness to distrust. I tried to backtrack, said something about the important role of the school, talked about the schools in France which were under the auspices of the church, but I failed to dispel the suspicion I had aroused.

Would you like another slice of pie? Jený asked, but Hermann looked at his watch, and said:

Well, time for me to go back to work.

Páll and I rose from the sofa.

It's snowing again, said Páll.

Yes, terrible weather we're having, said Jenný.

They accompanied us to the door, closing it the moment we started down the steps.

It was getting frostier inside than out, said Páll once we were sitting back in the car.

As we drove away, I noticed a face at the window and hoped I hadn't made an irrevocable mistake.

JESUS GAVE UP THE GHOST UP ON ÁRTÚNSBREKKA hill at the outskirts of Reykjavík. He had been making funny noises all morning, and Páll had decided to take him to a mechanic after we'd had a quick lunch. But we never made it all the way, for the engine started to stall on Miklabraut, and then died completely as we crossed the Elliðaár Rivers. Páll managed to steer Jesus off the road, so that at least we weren't blocking the traffic, and, as we stepped out, he said that he could even see the garage up on the hill. However, that didn't help very much.

Let's take a look at the engine, I said. We might be able to see what's going on.

He paused then leaned back inside the car.

I've never had to open the hood so I'm not even sure where the lever is, he said.

Try under the dashboard, I suggested.

At last he found it, and we checked the oil and water—or rather I did, for it appeared Páll had never seen an engine before. But I could find no obvious problem and asked him to turn the key in the ignition while I observed. At first I thought it might be a blockage in the fuel pump, but when the engine didn't even fire, it seemed more likely to be an electrical fault. I tried to explain this to Páll, but I lacked the necessary vocabulary to describe any of the parts. He simply shook his head.

The hood was still open when a truck pulled over, and the driver, an energetic-looking fellow, leapt out. He didn't try to hide his astonishment when he saw me poring over the engine, hands smeared with grease, but soon recovered his composure, asking Páll to turn the key in the ignition. Páll obliged and the truck driver was no less perplexed than I had been. As I outlined my theory about the electrical system, he listened, incredulous, examining me carefully. He looked as if it had suddenly occurred to him that I might be on my way to a costume party.

You mean the spark plugs and the ignition coil, he said at last. Possibly. Or it could be the crankshaft sensor, now that I think of it.

I jotted down the Icelandic words for *ignition coil* and *crankshaft sensor*, while committing *spark plug* to memory. I had started to note down words and expressions the moment I arrived in Iceland, because, of course, many of the words used in everyday speech were foreign to me. Sometimes, Páll would amuse himself by using phrases he knew would have me reaching for my pen—for example *to dig something*; as in: he doesn't dig it; or *nerd*—the guy is a total nerd; *guinea pig*; *dumbfounded*—and so on. I wrote everything down and then tried to make sentences using the expressions myself. It didn't always work out.

We waited while the car was being fixed. The owner of the garage, a middle-aged man, was as taken aback as the truck driver when he saw me step out of the tow truck but listened politely as I described the problem. When I uttered the words *spark plug, igni-*

tion coil, and *crankshaft sensor*, he looked inquiringly at Páll, who, half smiling, shrugged his shoulders.

Come to think of it, Páll was remarkably indifferent to the way people responded to us. I imagined that a young man like him would have found it rather awkward to be seen running around with a middle-aged nun, but nothing was further from the truth. He treated me as he would a good friend, whether alone or with others, and didn't seem the slightest bit embarrassed by our association.

For example, he was amused when the owner invited us into the lunchroom for a coffee, and the first thing that greeted us was a calendar on the wall above the table. The print was large and clear, as was the image—a comely young woman resting her weary bones beneath a palm tree on a sandy beach. Needless to say, in that heat she was scantily clad, and—momentarily at least—had removed her bra. The poor man only realized when it was too late, and although I pretended not to have noticed, he looked flustered for a moment then tore the calendar off the wall and hurried out.

Páll suppressed a giggle.

It's only normal for men to dream of the beach in winter, I said.

We helped ourselves to coffee out of a flask and sat down at the table. The canteen had two windows, one overlooking the parking lot behind the garage, the other the workshop itself. The car hood was open, and the garage owner, along with one other mechanic, was leaning over the engine.

I asked my father about him, Páll said, all of a sudden.

I beg your pardon?

Hermann Atlason. Last night. I forgot to tell you.

What did he say?

Not a lot, really. He said he only knows him to say hello to; apparently he and his wife are very active in the parish. I tried not to appear too interested, of course, just told him I had met them casually. However, it seems that more than once Hermann has quarreled with the staff in the Treasury Department and made himself a real nuisance. It was Mom who told me that. She says he's got the reputation of being quite pedantic.

I reached for my pad and jotted down the word once he had explained what it meant.

And the bishop couldn't tell you anything about the family?

No, the truth is he doesn't remember Hermann, only Jenný. He ought to be better acquainted with the congregation by now, but he doesn't seem all that interested. He's an academic. He prefers the company of books.

The car had been hoisted up. I watched the two men for a while as they fumbled underneath the engine.

What do we do next? asked Páll. I doubt we'll get any more out of Hermann or Jenný. Or Karólína Símonardóttir.

I nodded in agreement, and he waited for me to suggest our next steps.

What do you suppose they're looking for? I said, thinking out loud.

Who?

The mechanics. They're looking under the chassis.

He glanced toward the workshop.

It's probably the carburetor, he said.

The carburetor?

Yes, it must be.

Are you out of your mind? The carburetor . . .

I caught on when I saw his expression and stopped in midsentence. He was grinning from ear to ear.

That's practically the only engine part I can name, he said.

I laughed at him, and at myself, too, of course, but I also scolded myself for the fastidious tone in my voice. Then he mimicked me, just for fun: The carburetor?

An hour later we drove off having been told that the spark plugs were shot and the brake pads needed renewing. It had started to snow and was getting dark.

What do we do now? he asked again.

I think it's time we paid a visit to the school, I said.

He was silent.

Do you think it might be better if you go on your own? he said at last.

His change of tone took me by surprise. I thought I glimpsed traces of an old fear, helplessness and self-doubt. As if he were suddenly that little boy again, summoned before the headmaster because of poor performance, or some minor mischief.

We'll go together, I said. You needn't worry.

I SOMETIMES WONDER WHETHER RAFFIN WOULD HAVE left me alone had I not been so prideful. Had I behaved toward him as Halla did, engaged in small talk, given him the attention he clearly sought, flattered his vanity. Did I bring misfortune upon myself, I wonder, when I'm feeling blue, should I have humbled myself, let him go on believing that he was superior to us, ignored him? I wonder whether I didn't perhaps expose my mind to him through my behavior and make things easier for him through my defiance—in other words, whether I have only myself to blame.

Such thoughts are hardly healthy. One thing leads to another, the journey is punctuated by chance, by fortune and misfortune. A sudden frost after careful sowing, the fruit turns sour, the leaves fall from the trees. And yet we try to follow our conscience, to do our best, to do unto others as we would have them do unto us, to contribute. Not in the hope of a better place after this one, of impressing others or even ourselves, but rather because that is what makes us happiest, enables us to face each new day fearlessly, to lie down at night with our shadow, as I recall Saint Benedict put it, to sleep with peace in our hearts.

I did my best to push Raffin away and make him understand

that I wanted nothing to do with him. Perhaps I went too far. I was convinced, for example, that he was only trying to harass me when he started to make regular visits to the reading room, which up until then Halla and I had mainly had to ourselves. I didn't try to hide how I felt. Let's go, I said to her on two occasions, when we opened the door and found him ensconced in the armchair next to the window. I turned on my heels and shut the door behind us, but the expression in his eyes stayed with me—mocking the first time, cold the second. Or at least so I imagined afterward.

He caught me off guard when he finally approached me. It was just before Easter; Halla had gone to Berlin to meet a cousin of hers. The guesthouse was busy, but I had encouraged her to go, promising to stand in for her, even though I had plenty of assignments and a long essay to hand in after the holiday.

He made his move on Holy Thursday, after Matins. I was minding my own business, on my way back to the guesthouse from the basilica when I noticed him approach out of the corner of my eye. I continued on my way, never for a moment suspecting that he wanted to talk to me, but stopped dead in my tracks when I suddenly felt a hand on my shoulders.

I need to speak with you.

I was about to brush him off with a curt reply, but something in his voice made me hesitate. Although I had the perfect excuse of my morning chores, rather than ignoring him, I followed him into the small nook set aside for the deacons.

Have a seat.

I did as he said. He sat down opposite me, put down the prayer book he was still carrying from Matins.

I find myself in a difficult situation, he began, and I'm not sure what to do. On the one hand I am tempted to do nothing, but temptation being what it is, the consequences are never good. And yet I do not wish to cause harm—we all find refuge in love, as the saying goes, and all I want is to help people. That is how I have tried to live my life, although I am as flawed as the next man.

He spoke deliberately, as might an old person, in a detached but amiable voice, a look of compassion on his face. Later on, of course, I realized it had all been an act, the speech thoroughly rehearsed, his facial expressions meticulously planned.

He leaned forward, rocking in his seat, clasping and unclasping his fingers.

But where does friendship end and recklessness begin? What are our duties toward our brothers and sisters, toward our own conscience, and toward God himself? This is what I have been racking my brains about recently, without much success, to my dismay.

And yet, as always, the answer is in the Holy Scriptures. I think you know this yourself, Pauline, otherwise you would not have come here. You would not have chosen to study theology at the Sorbonne or to take lodgings with the nuns here at the guesthouse. We all have our demons, and you better than anyone know that you must rid yourself of yours.

I sat motionless, unable to speak. All my defiance had evaporated, and a feeling of fear filled my whole being. I realized I was shaking.

You are doubtless familiar with Paul's words in his epistle to the Romans, and also in his First Epistle to the Corinthians, so I needn't remind you of them.

Yes, of course I knew them by heart and had tortured myself for years thinking about them.

". . . women exchanged natural sexual relations for unnatural ones, and have been justly punished for their sins . . . Or do you not know that wrongdoers will not inherit the kingdom of God? Neither the sexually immoral nor idolaters nor adulterers nor men who have sex with other men."

I lowered my gaze, but he went on.

Halla is a good girl. I fear for her, because clearly you have no self-control. I was saddened when she told me that you had found an excuse to sneak into her bed at night. I realized then that I must take matters into my own hands.

Of course Halla hadn't said those words. Of course she hadn't told him that I had used the pretext of the cold weather or suggested anything untoward. And yet I felt exposed, unable to defend myself.

I want to help you, I heard him say, but you must change your ways. You are capable of it, you are strong, and I know you care about the state of your soul. About your reputation. There is no need to inform your nearest and dearest—your family, your colleagues at work, your friends, Halla. No need at all, providing you turn over a new leaf, and seek refuge in our Savior.

He fell silent, and I thought he had finished. I tried to choke back my sobs, and nearly succeeded, although the tears were streaming down my face. I heard him rise from his chair and walk over to me, but I didn't look up. Then he placed his hand on the back of my head, let it rest there, and said:

You must leave here. Both for your own and for Halla's sake. You cannot remain here any longer.

THE TELEPHONE DIRECTORY. I MENTIONED IT TO PÁLL on the way back from the garage.

Who are you looking for?

I gazed out the window, trying to sound nonchalant.

I met a young Icelandic woman about twenty years ago in Paris. We were at the Sorbonne together. She isn't in the directory.

What's her name?

Halla Hjartardóttir.

He thought for a while then said:

No, the name doesn't ring a bell.

I couldn't help smiling. He must have noticed and added by way of explanation:

There aren't that many of us in Iceland. Is she your age?

Slightly younger. She must be about forty by now. In fact, it was her birthday on December 4.

He glanced at me, and I feared I had said too much. But, of course, I soon realized I was being foolish.

The same day as my brother Gunnar.

To be polite, I asked him about his brother; he was three years younger and studying engineering. Then he asked me:

Where does she live?

I don't know.

Not in Reykjavík?

She did twenty years ago, but I have no idea if she does now. For all I know she could have moved abroad.

When did you last hear from her?

I paused.

About twenty years ago.

After Easter, I moved into a small apartment not far from the guesthouse. It was owned by the church and intended to house visiting nuns. Raffin had arranged for me to move in even before he spoke to me, taking advantage of the fact that the young woman who lived with the nuns and looked after the apartment had resigned and left. Those days are a blur, but I will never forget packing my clothes, books, and meager belongings, before saying good-bye to the room Halla and I had shared. I remember sitting on her bed, pressing her pillow to my face, opening the wardrobe, and seeing her before me dressed in the clothes that hung inside. I resisted touching them, but paused with my suitcase in the doorway, before closing the door behind me.

I felt as if one of us had died. I just didn't know which.

Are you sure she's still alive? asked Páll.

I had been avoiding thinking about that possibility, and I gave a start. He noticed, adding: I'm just saying. We can easily find out.

How?

By looking in the national archive. We can stop by there now if you want. Then, assuming she is still alive, we can also find out where she lives.

No, I said.

Are you sure?

Yes, not now. We have enough on our plate as it is.

I bumped into Halla in the refectory the day after she returned from Berlin. She hurried over as soon as she saw me come in.

What happened? she asked. You never told me you were moving out.

I told her that I was offered the job unexpectedly and couldn't turn it down, because in addition to free food and lodgings, I would receive a small salary. I had rehearsed a more expansive reply, but those few words were all I could muster. Of course, the ensuing silence spoke more than my fabricated story, and it was Halla who broke it:

Is something wrong?

No, nothing, I said, and tried to change the subject, asking her how her trip went, whether Berlin was an interesting city, and a few other questions in that vein.

We sat down with our food at our usual table. I didn't see Raffin, but I could feel his eyes on me and was on my guard. Obviously, Halla knew that something wasn't right and asked again what the matter was. Once more I insisted that everything was fine, but my voice rang hollow, my gestures were awkward, as though I had taken on a role that I couldn't play.

Gradually, we drifted apart, until we only met in the refectory. I stopped going to dance class, on the pretext of being too busy with my new job, my Icelandic classes fell by the wayside, and our shared moments in the reading room ended. I was half hoping she would be angry with me and even give me an earful, but that wasn't her nature. She seemed dreadfully sad, which was what hurt me the most.

Raffin kept a close eye on me. We didn't speak very often, but occasionally he would make his presence felt. You're doing well, he would say, in that fatherly tone which I couldn't stand. Adding as he took his leave: God bless you. Those words coming from his lips felt like being lashed with a whip.

One afternoon, in the middle of May, Halla was waiting for me outside the main entrance to the college. It was four o'clock, and my last lecture had just finished. As I came out, I saw her immediately in the quadrangle. She was facing the other way, and I stood still watching her. It occurred to me to flee back into the building and leave by a different exit, but instead I walked toward her, slowly, suppressing the urge to run over and fling my arms about her.

We said hello. I tried to smile.

The weather is getting warmer, I said, because at last spring was in the air and the clouds that had hung over the city for the past few days had evaporated.

We sauntered off, chatting about everything except for the thing that really mattered to us—the weather, college, a nun who had broken her leg earlier that week, the food at the guesthouse, which we both agreed had gotten worse lately. I even forgot myself for an instant, perhaps becoming more like my old self, because all at once she came to a halt, grabbed my arm, and said:

Pauline, have I done something wrong?

At first I couldn't speak. We had stopped, and I glanced

around, looking left and right, as though searching for an answer, until I sighed: No, you've done nothing wrong.

I was on the verge of explaining everything to her. About Father Raffin, his insinuations, the power he had over me, the conditions he had laid down. But at the last moment, I thought better of it, because that would have meant telling her my innermost thoughts. And I couldn't do that, even though it would have been healthiest for me and might even have released me from the spell. That is what I tell myself now when I look back, after going over it in my mind countless times, without always coming to the same conclusion.

No, you haven't done anything. The post suddenly became available, and apart from the salary, it is good for me to live more closely with nuns. In fact, I'm thinking of taking my vows.

I was telling the truth, although I had never given it any thought before Raffin passed judgment on me. I wouldn't say I took the decision calmly, but rather that I was driven to it by despair. I felt I had nowhere else to turn and was unable to envision living a so-called normal life, in harmony with others and myself. I must not love; for my love was a crime against God and man, and the punishment was excommunication. The most I could do for this young woman whom I loved more than anyone in the world, more than myself, was to silence my feelings for her, to expunge myself from her life.

I told myself in a moment of rare clarity that perhaps I would find freedom in faith, but then my thoughts would cloud over again, and I would convince myself that I had to stand up to God and his servants, break into his citadel and speak out for those who were suffering, for myself and other outcasts.

Halla looked at me, surprised.

Are you serious? A nun?

I nodded. She stood still, and I was expecting her to smile and wish me well. But she didn't; indeed, my announcement appeared to have wounded her. I was puzzled and thought about elaborating when she seemed to collect herself.

I'm sorry, she said. You just took me by surprise.

We walked home in silence. When we parted, she said: I'm so very fond of you.

I was going to echo her words, yet my tongue wouldn't move. When at last my mind rallied, she had turned around, and was hurrying across the road toward the steps of the Sacré-Coeur.

I slept little that night and rushed over to breakfast at the guesthouse, for I couldn't wait to see her. Perhaps I was going to say something to her, I don't know, my thoughts were in turmoil. But her demeanor had changed completely, her old smile was back, and that ease that bordered on indifference.

A fortnight after term finished, she returned to Iceland. She had only planned to stay in Paris for a year, although I had hoped she might change her mind and more than once suggested that her French was now so fluent that she could probably complete her degree here. But of course that was before Raffin appeared on the scene, and anyway it was by no means certain that staying was ever an option.

I met her in the refectory that morning, and then helped her pack. I hadn't been in our room since I moved out and was unprepared for the memories it brought back. I could see us so clearly before me, when things were going our way, when nothing threatened to mar our happiness. I could hear our voices when we were tucked up in bed, after we turned out the lights, our laughter and whispers, and also the silence, when we sat on our separate beds, absorbed in our books, trying to concentrate on our studies, or when, all at once we decided to take a break and listen to a Beatles' song, for example, "Michelle," which remained one of our favorites.

But those memories evaporated, and I found myself staring at her as she stood in the middle of the room glancing around, bewildered, I thought.

I think that's everything.

I was close to breaking down, but managed to contain myself, and to say an Icelandic word she had taught me had many different nuances:

Jæja. Well, well.

She couldn't help smiling, and I smiled back, and for an instant I felt sure one of us would say something else, but neither of us did.

I helped her out with her suitcases. The caretaker at the Sacré-Coeur had offered to drive her to the airport, and we went around to where he parked his Citroën next to the side door of the church. He gave us a friendly greeting, put the suitcases in the trunk, and climbed into the driver's seat.

I don't know how long we stood there, staring into each other's eyes. Sometimes, when I look back, it seems like forever. The morning sun shone on one side of her face, the other was in shadow. She was wearing an orange scarf around her neck.

Jæja.

We said nothing as we embraced, although a strange shiver went through me. I held her tight; hoping somehow to convey to her what was taking place inside me; clasped her to me, but again was unable to utter a word.

The caretaker started the car. We relaxed our embrace, tentatively.

She opened the passenger door, and I thought she was going to climb in, when suddenly she wheeled around and grabbed at my hands. She didn't look at me, but we held hands for a moment, before she closed the car door behind her.

I watched them drive away. The Citroën was bright green and jolted slightly. The sun went on shining.

I stood still for a long time after they had disappeared, eyes closed, as I tried to fix in my memory our last caress.

HILDUR, THE BISHOP'S SECRETARY, CONTACTED THE headmaster to set up a meeting. When I asked Páll what exactly had been said, he didn't know.

I'm not sure whether she mentioned anything about the reason for your visit, he said. She simply asked him to receive you at the bishop's request.

Didn't she tell him anything about me?

I doubt it. I expect she kept the conversation brief. She hasn't much time for Father August Frans. Don't ask me why.

We were sitting in the living room at Ljósvallagata. I hadn't slept well and was feeling tired. Páll could tell.

I had made us some tea. It was almost one o'clock, and I had just had my lunch of bread and pickled herring, which I bought from the local grocery store on the corner. Father August Frans had agreed to see me at two o'clock when the school day was winding down. The sky was overcast, the snow had started to thaw, the air was damp and chilly.

That morning, I had watched men digging a grave in the cemetery across the street. Looking out now, I saw a hearse draw up outside the cemetery. The grave was close to the street, and the bearers carried the casket toward it along a narrow path that had just been cleared of snow. The funeral director ushered them to the graveside, after which the priest took over the proceedings. The living room window was open, and I could hear the murmur of the burial service and the song that followed, an old Icelandic psalm, according to Páll.

"Just as the perfect bloom . . ."

We stood by the window; everything was black and white and gray, just like on the old television set in the apartment, which hadn't yet been replaced with a new color one. I asked him about funeral services in Iceland, and he gave me a detailed account, mentioning various rites that didn't exist in Catholicism.

Don't you think it might be more effective if you go there on your own, he then said out of the blue.

I watched the casket descend into the ground.

". . . Sheds its colors and leaves, so human life ends too soon."

You needn't come if you don't want to, I said, but who knows, it might do you some good.

We left it at that and shortly after we went out to the car. Jesus had perked up after his visit to the mechanic, was quicker to start than before, and the occasional hiccup we had been noticing in recent days had disappeared. His acceleration seemed better, and I had the distinct impression he was eager to take us to our destination. There was ice on the roads, but Páll drove more slowly than he needed to, and when at last we arrived at the school, I calculated we would have gotten there quicker on foot.

He left the engine running, and I waited for a few seconds before making to open the door. It was exactly two o'clock. We hadn't spoken much on the way, but it was obvious that Páll was engaged in an intense dialogue with himself. This appeared to have come to an end when he switched off the ignition and declared, decisively, as if to steel himself:

I'm coming with you.

The path up to the school was slippery, and we took it slowly. I felt a fine spray on my cheeks, and I paused to look up at the dark church tower, which seemed farther away in the mist. I had been lax about attending prayers and felt ashamed of myself.

The first thing I noticed when we entered the school was how quiet it was inside. There were a few children in the corridors, on their way from one classroom to another, I assumed, or to the adjacent gym, yet they avoided making any noise, speaking in whispers and terribly well behaved, except for two boys who couldn't help themselves, tossing a ball between them as they approached the main door. I moved to the side, so as not to get in their way, but also because I enjoyed watching their eager, glowing faces, as their cheerfulness was almost contagious. As they approached me, they suddenly stopped dead in their tracks. Their smiles faded, and the one with the ball clasped it tight to ensure he wouldn't drop it. Both boys lowered their heads as they walked past us with slow, cautious steps, before vanishing quietly through the door.

I couldn't understand what had frightened them until I looked over my shoulder and saw a middle-aged woman standing in the doorway of a room next to the main entrance. She wore a black skirt and a gray blouse and was glowering at Páll and me. I was about to introduce myself, when she cut in.

Father August Frans is waiting for you, she said, then glancing at her wristwatch, she added: You're late.

She motioned to us to follow her to the headmaster's office, and we silently obeyed. During the short walk, she did not once look over her shoulder or address us. She knocked on the door and turned the handle at the same time, leaving us standing outside as she pulled the door closed behind her.

Páll and I looked at each other. It didn't surprise me that he was a little uneasy, as I myself felt like I was back at primary school and had been summoned to see Sister Josephine, who was in the habit of scolding us students for the smallest infraction.

Miss Stein, whispered Páll. Always like a bright ray of sunshine.

Presently the door opened again, only this time we were confronted with the headmaster himself, a small man in a gray suit wearing horn-rimmed spectacles, not quite hunched over, but slightly stooped, his thinning hair scraped across his head.

But it was his eyes that struck me the most, his smile and his eyes narrowing to the point where they were barely visible.

Sister Johanna?

We greeted each other, and he ushered us—or should I say me—in, for he pretended not to have noticed poor Páll, who seemed to shrivel up with every second. I probably should have overlooked this, left Páll to disappear into the shadows, where he would doubtless have felt better, but then I would have been giving Father August Frans the upper hand, and I didn't propose to start the meeting on that footing.

You two already know each other, of course, I said, standing aside so that Páll couldn't hide behind me, and Father August Frans would be forced to acknowledge him.

The priest continued to smile.

Of course, he said. Páll, welcome to your old school.

He installed himself behind his desk, while we sat on two chairs facing him. The glowering Miss Stein was nowhere to be seen, having likely left through a painted door, which I noticed between two tall bookcases on the south-facing wall. I glanced out the window overlooking the church. The mist had turned to heavy rain.

Welcome to Iceland, Sister Johanna.

Thank you.

Have you enjoyed your stay?

Yes, although I've only just arrived and am still getting my bearings.

As am I, he said, and I've been here almost a quarter of a century.

He continued to smile, and I smiled back, wishing I was more prepared, had worked out how I would direct the conversation and better acquainted myself with the headmaster's personality. I confess that I was unnerved by his smile, which seemed out of context and suggested nothing to me about the man's feelings or his character, possibly because his eyes, tiny slits behind his spectacles, gave nothing away; they certainly weren't windows into his soul, which seemed carefully concealed behind them.

That is a long time, I said at last. Did you come straight here to the school, or did you first take up a position in the church?

I was asked to take over as headmaster of the school, he said, and that is why I came to Iceland. Of course, I have also been working for the church all these years, as I expect you are aware, contributed what I could. What about you, Sister Johanna? What brings you to these shores in the middle of winter?

I cleared my throat softly, agreed that this was certainly not the ideal time of year and added that, as in his case, it was God's intention that I embark upon this journey, and therefore I had no choice but to obey.

I saw Páll cast me a sidelong glance, for he hadn't heard me speak in this tone before. For I was using as my script Raffin's words when he advised me about how to reveal the nature of my assignment; I recited my lines exactly as I had memorized them, changing my voice accordingly, my speech taking on a formal air, which distanced me from myself and emboldened me at the same time.

Our brothers at the Vatican have entrusted me with a small assignment, I said. They wish to assess the running of the church's schools all over the world, not least in far-flung places. I had therefore come to Iceland on a fact-finding mission and was obliged to him for receiving me.

Then I take it that you have experience in education? he said.

I taught a little when I was younger, I said. But it was my knowledge of the language that persuaded them to send me here.

And what would you like to know about our school? he asked, settling back in his chair.

He didn't wait for me to reply, but carried on talking: We have eight teachers, just over a hundred pupils. We teach them to read and write, to do arithmetic; we teach Christian studies, history, geography, biology, and handicrafts. We also have a small gym next door. We strive to graduate them with more knowledge than when they arrived, to prepare them for life, to mold them as best we can. It really is as simple as that, Sister Johanna.

He spoke in a detached voice with that smile on his lips. There was no trace of irony in his voice, on the contrary, and he seemed almost surprised that anyone could be interested in such a simple, dull occupation. And indeed, he went on to say:

We are like Sisyphus, Sister Johanna, we push the boulder up the hill by day, only to watch it roll back down at night. The next morning, we start again.

His smile seemed to widen, even as his eyes narrowed still more.

What about the church's role in the school? I asked. In what way do they contribute?

He reflected for a moment.

We cannot complain, although some might say that their support hasn't been very forthcoming. Some might say that we have been left to run the school on our own, without any help from them at all. Indeed, I was hoping you might have come here to change that. You are presumably aware of the petitions we have made, and the replies we received?

No, I said.

Really?

I shook my head and told myself that it wouldn't have hurt Raffin to prepare me better.

For the most part, our requests were denied, he said. And it was left up to us to find ways of funding the school. But with God's blessing we've been able to do that, so we cannot complain.

I had no idea, I said.

There is so much that we do not know, Sister Johanna. Sometimes it's as if we are in a hall of mirrors, unable to tell which way is up, and which way down, for everything is distorted, nothing is what it seems. I was hoping you had come here bearing gifts and good news, yet you see how mistaken I was.

I was relieved when he looked at his watch. We rose from our seats, and I thanked him for his time.

The least I could do, he said, following us out into the corridor. And of course you must continue to get to know the congregation, to meet people like Hermann and Jenný.

I was taken aback but tried not to let it show.

The salt of the earth, he went on. Reliable, hardworking, honest folk.

I felt the urge to quicken my pace toward the exit, but I checked myself. Páll, on the other hand, had difficulty, and was striding ahead when all of a sudden the priest waylaid him.

Páll, my dear boy, what news of our bishop?

Everything's fine, Páll gasped.

Do you think he might emerge from his study anytime soon?

Páll stammered, but fortunately by then we had reached the main entrance. Father August Frans reached for the handle and opened the door for us.

It's getting dark already, he said. The Icelandic winters aren't for everyone, Sister Johanna.

We took our leave. Unfortunately, the ice prevented me from fleeing that place as fast as I would have liked.

ROSES ARE HARDIER PLANTS THAN MOST PEOPLE realize, and it's not as if I am the only person in the world who knows how to care for them. Still I can't help worrying.

By this I am not implying that I have no faith in Sister Marie Joseph. I went over the rota with her so many times before my departure that I imagine she was getting a little tired of me by the end. She has been my apprentice for about a year, assisting me on a regular basis and learning everything I am able to teach her. I also left a detailed list of instructions, which I wrote out over the weekend, just to avoid any mishaps or confusion. She can be a little dreamy and is apt to forget herself, and although I am sure my roses can withstand a minor upset, I can't help thinking about all the things that could go wrong.

In any event, the beginning of summer has been better than expected, and it is no exaggeration to say that most of the roses are thriving. The winter months were hard, and toward the end I was afraid that some of them might not survive, particularly the rambling roses that grow amid the ruins of the old cowshed. The walls that remain face north and west, and offer good shelter, yet for some reason the stems along those walls suffered the worst frost damage. We had to cut a lot of them away, and I showed Marie Joseph how best to prune the stems without damaging the emerging buds. She did a thorough job, and I made sure to praise her regularly, although I confess that I was probably breathing too much down her neck. Not that she seemed to mind; on the contrary, she chattered away as she worked, quizzing me about the different varieties of rose, asking me to explain their nature and behavior, and retaining more than I ever expected.

More than once, she asked me what my favorite roses were, but I always replied that I couldn't choose between them. Once, I said that the roses were my children, or words to the effect, and then her face took on a strange, rather sad expression. It occurred to me that without meaning to I had reminded her that she herself would never have children. She soon regained her cheerfulness, declaring that the two she found most beautiful were the tea roses, Gloire de Dijon and Monsieur Tillier. I took the opportunity to tell her where the name *tea rose* came from—possibly at greater length than was necessary. She appeared to listen with interest, and yet I thought I could still glimpse a trace of sorrow in her eyes.

But enough of that, the roses have, without exception, survived the winter and the two cold snaps at the end of April and the beginning of May. Some of them even started flowering two weeks early and show no signs of slowing down, but are working hard to delight our senses. Old Madame de la Roche-Lambert has surprised me, as has the newest rose, Traviata, from the nursery at Meilland, which seems impervious to blight, and is also a repeat bloomer, holding its own among the august ladies, some of whom have lived here for decades. I find it has an apple scent, and I said so to Marie Joseph, who completely agreed with me.

And yet, I worry that I didn't stress enough the importance of some of the items on my list. I ought to have gone to the stationery store down in the village and made a photocopy of it to take with me, because now I cannot recall the details. And God is always in the details, which I have been striving to master from the first day I began looking after the rose garden.

I am standing in front of the Sacré-Coeur. It is almost six o'clock. I have been dillydallying here since I took my leave of the young couple, some ten minutes ago. Perhaps I am imagining that I was of some help to them, perhaps it is merely wishful thinking, yet I can confirm they were smiling and holding hands so tenderly when they left that it warmed my heart.

I had fully intended to visit the guesthouse, but now I am of two minds. *What have I to gain from it?* I ask myself. *Doesn't that building already occupy too much space in my head?*

I look toward the guesthouse and the convent, shifting slightly sideways so that I glimpse the window in the reading room. But then my thoughts return to the rose garden, the doubts that have been plaguing me since I was on the train, and which only increased in the basilica, when I should have been conversing with God. I pluck the phone out of my bag and reflect on how I can word my instructions so as not to offend Sister Marie Joseph.

WE SHOULD HAVE EXPECTED HERMANN TO GET in touch with Father August Frans, said Páll when we met the day after our visit to the headmaster.

I couldn't disagree.

But I'm not sure that it changed anything, he added. He would still have been on his guard.

Earlier that morning, on our way to church, I had discussed the school with the German nuns. One of them had been to Iceland twice before and already knew Father August Frans. She had only good things to say about him. Obviously, I couldn't tell them anything about the nature of my business here, but her admiration for him was palpable.

I was thrown into confusion, no longer sure of myself, and I started to doubt the truth of the anonymous letter that had set everything in motion. I kept thinking about his smile. I could find in it neither warmth nor mockery, and the same went for his scarcely visible eyes. I considered what my impression of him might have been had I not read the accusations in the letter and wondered whether I hadn't prejudged the man before I even met him.

Although I didn't exactly find the answers to my questions, I concluded that the most honorable course of action would have been to go to him first, before looking elsewhere, to have shown him the letter and let him defend himself. Perhaps there was a simple explanation, perhaps he could have dispelled these suspicions in an instant, clarified matters, put them in their natural context.

It was as if Páll had read my thoughts, for all at once he blurted: I don't trust him.

But does that mean he is guilty?

I don't know, he said.

I told him about the German nun, her account of the mass taken by Father August Frans, which she had attended during one of her visits.

His Gregorian chant was memorable, she said, when he began reciting the Nicene Creed: *Credo in unum Deum* . . . There was an inherent beauty and purity to his voice.

I pride myself on being able to read people's spirit through their song, I told Páll, aware of how shallow my claim might sound. I have never heard a wicked person sing beautifully, not noticeably in any case . . .

I've never heard him sing, he replied. And I wasn't aware that he took mass.

We were sitting outside Bishop Johnson's office waiting for him to return from lunch. He had summoned us to a meeting on short notice, but Páll had no idea why he wanted to see us. The bishop hadn't spoken about any subsequent meetings when I saw him the day after I arrived, nor had he asked me to keep him informed of my progress—on the contrary, he seemed to want as little as possible to do with me and my mission. And yet there we were outside his office, speculating about what was on his mind.

He soon appeared, apologized for being late, and took off his overcoat, which he handed to his secretary who hung it in the closet. We followed him through to his office.

Are you getting anywhere? he asked, as we seated ourselves around the coffee table. He was his usual polite self, and yet there was a touch of impatience in his voice that took me by surprise.

We are still in the early stages, I replied.

He cleared his throat.

Have you any proof that these accusations are based in fact?

We haven't gotten far enough yet to prove or disprove anything, I said.

He leaned back in his chair.

I had an extremely difficult conversation with Father August Frans this morning.

I waited for him to go on.

Regarding the history of the school's finances. He felt the need to recall various details about which I know nothing, having only recently taken up my post. Indeed, I said as much to him. Even so, he insisted, adopting an unnecessarily forceful attitude with me. How could I possibly defend something that happened before my time?

I have no idea if he realized how unclear he sounded. In fact, I had the impression that he was talking to himself rather than to Páll and me, who were doing our best to fill in the blanks. I took the opportunity when the bishop paused to ask him in what way their conversation and our meeting with the headmaster were related.

Then he finally explained to me that Father August Frans was under the impression that I had been sent to redress the church's failings, which he considered disgraceful. From the beginning it had been understood that the church supported the school, both spiritually and financially. That was what he had been promised when he was offered the post, and to begin with the church had kept its word, not as generously as he would have liked, but enough to save face. Soon, however, they had started to drag their heels, and in recent years the situation had deteriorated to the point where he had become wholly responsible for funding the school, because the church had done nothing, given him the runaround, left him high and dry.

The bishop paused, and for a moment I wasn't sure whether he was blaming me or looking for sympathy. But then he sighed and said:

What on earth made him think that you came here to discuss the school's finances with him and redress the situation?

Páll and I glanced at each other.

I told Father August Frans I was here simply to assess the running of the church's schools.

The running of the church's schools? And by so doing you acknowledged that the school is the church's responsibility. Is it any surprise that he seized upon it?

I assured the bishop that it was Father August Frans who had brought up the subject of money.

He gave another sigh, leaned back in his chair, then rose to his feet and went over to the window.

Didn't you tell him about the letter?

No.

You didn't mention it at all?

I thought it unwise to bring that up at our first meeting.

Perhaps you are right, he said, and I was tempted to remind

him that he himself had been quick to forward the letter to the Vatican, but I thought better of it.

So, despite having spoken to Father August Frans and to the boys' parents, you have gotten nowhere.

I had to admit that I'd made little headway.

Sister Johanna, you have some experience in these matters. Do you believe there is any truth in these accusations?

I hesitated, and, perhaps needn't have said anything, for the doubts I was starting to have must have been written all over my face. Even so, I replied, more softly than I had intended:

I don't know.

You've met the parties concerned, and yet you're none the wiser. This must stop. We cannot let all hell break loose because of one letter we know next to nothing about, not even who wrote it.

I said that I understood.

So can we end the matter there?

No, I need more time.

A few more days, Sister Johanna, until the weekend at the latest, and for heaven's sake try to avoid any controversy.

PÁLL HAD LOOKED AT ME WHEN BISHOP JOHNSON mentioned my previous experience. In fact, he had given me a sidelong glance whenever he thought his boss was asking an awkward question, but in that instance I was more aware of his eyes on me.

I sensed it again once we were in the car. Although he said nothing, I was sure that he was wondering what that experience was. Perhaps he was thinking that it must have been flimsy, given what I had achieved so far. He hadn't been able to draw me out before and was resisting asking again. Or so I imagined.

He's all stressed out, he declared instead.

I said something about the bishop obviously being under pressure.

It doesn't sit well with him, he said. He hates any kind of discord.

Páll went down Hávallagata toward Garðastræti, turned left, and drove along slowly. We hadn't talked about where we were going, and I had no plans yet.

What shall we do now? he asked, in a tone that didn't sound as if he expected me to have an answer ready.

We drove through the town in silence, around Lake Tjörnin,

then out to the shore. My surroundings were beginning to look familiar; the center is quite small, and it's a short drive out to the suburbs. The sea was rough, the sky above steely gray, and snow-flakes swirled in the wind that buffeted the car. Páll came to a halt. We gazed out at the ocean. On the radio someone was reading a serialized story, which neither of us had noticed until now.

A recent novel, said Páll. About a sailor who has difficulty finding his footing on land.

We listened for a while. The sailor's wife told him she wanted a divorce. He appeared resigned and didn't try to talk her out of it.

You wanted to know about my previous case, I said.

He waited.

There is a reason why I don't talk about it much.

Of course, I understand, it's confidential.

The reason is that I didn't do a good job.

I turned the radio down, without switching it off. I hadn't thought about what I would share with Páll, and what I would keep to myself, I simply followed my instinct. In brief, I mentioned very little about Raffin, and nothing about our dealings, how we got to know each other, the power he wielded over me. Nor did I mention Halla, or my feelings for her, but rather I focused on the situation itself, without holding anything back.

I saw very little of Raffin after Halla's departure. He was soon given his first parish, in northern France, Brittany to be exact, and I also moved, to the convent in the nineteenth arrondissement. I hoped I would never see him again, but I didn't feel at peace and sensed his presence without reason.

It was only upon my return from Africa when I settled at Saint-Amand-Montrond that I discovered he had been a priest there for nearly four years. To begin with I felt disheartened, but then the anger welled up inside me. But I had no opportunity to vent my feelings, because he ignored me pretty much, even on the few occasions when he visited the convent. It was Sister Marie Agnès, recently appointed Mother Superior, who received him then. She was so impressed with him and spoke of him with such admiration that it was difficult to listen to.

Ostensibly, he came to speak to her, not me, about a priest in the next town. Afterward, she informed me that the archbishop of Bourges himself had assigned an important mission to Raffin. Clearly, she knew little about it and was simply repeating what Raffin had told her. She spoke about allegations of misconduct and so forth, which all sounded rather vague.

He needs assistance and he specifically mentioned you, Sister Johanna. He told me that you had shown great inner strength during a difficult situation when you were in Paris . . .

I agreed to meet him, because she was inquisitive, and I wanted to end the conversation as quickly as possible.

The next day, I drove down to the village in the Renault's predecessor—a yellow Citroën that was on its last legs at the time. Raffin received me in the church and went straight to the point. He didn't bring up the past, doubtless because he considered it unnecessary.

He informed me that the priest in question had been accused of behaving inappropriately toward a young boy. The lad's mother claimed that this behavior had been going on for several years, and that her son wasn't the only victim. He also told me that he had spoken with the mother and her son, who was unforthcoming, as well as with the priest, who denied everything and was shocked.

The priest claimed that since losing her husband that winter, the boy's mother hadn't been herself. He had tried to help her, but to no avail. According to him, she held God responsible.

In the past, I might have said "understandably," but this time I held my tongue and asked what he wanted from me.

He said that he had considered the matter closed, because he had no proof of the priest's guilt, and the mother's word wasn't enough; she hadn't even been able to persuade her own son to speak out, let alone the parents of the other boys, whom she claimed had also been abused.

I informed her of my decision yesterday, Raffin continued. She took it badly. After much reflection, I agreed to her request—or rather to her demand—that a woman speak to her son. She maintains that, due to his experiences, he has a mistrust of priests . . . And that this is why I could get nothing out of him.

Why me? I was going to ask, but stopped myself, perhaps fearing his reply. Even so, as he continued, he answered my question, nominally at least.

This isn't such an onerous task, he said. And there aren't many people around here to whom I could turn. You're a woman of the world.

His words hung in the air. I thought I understood his meaning, though his expression gave nothing away.

I visited the mother and her son later that day. I should of course have prepared myself better, but Raffin insisted I get together with them as soon as possible. Apart from that, he was circumspect, suggesting it was best I make up my own mind, independently of what he or others might think.

The mother worked at a pharmacy. I picked her up there and

drove her back to her house. They lived close by, on the second floor in a new apartment building. Through the living room windows, you could see the sand mines to the west of the town.

Her son was at home. Father Raffin had insisted I speak to him alone, which his mother immediately agreed to.

He was twelve years old, small for his age, dark-haired, but pale and withdrawn. We went to sit in the living room while his mother waited in the kitchen. I asked him about school, and football, although I knew little about the sport, and so I didn't recognize the team shirt he was wearing.

Nantes, he said in a hushed voice.

Are you a fan?

Yes.

Do you play much football?

No.

He looked down at his lap and continued to reply to my questions with a yes or a no or with an occasional "I don't know." I sensed how awkward he felt and realized that I wasn't making much progress with this chitchat, so I decided to get to the point.

Do you know what your mummy has been saying about Father Desbois?

He seemed to shrink into himself even more, but after a brief hesitation, he nodded.

Is this true?

Silence. I could hear the heavy machinery at the sand mine.

You can trust me, I said.

He raised his eyes for the first time and looked straight at me.

You won't tell anyone?

I wavered. If I said no, I would be unable to betray his confidence, and Father Desbois would be free of all charges. If I told him that I was obliged to report our conversation, then I risked him remaining silent.

And that was exactly what happened, when at last I replied. He stood up, opened the door, and walked out. I told his mother what had passed between us, and although she was upset, she showed both common sense and compassion. She went to the boy's room, and I saw her put her arms around him and draw him to her. I quietly saw myself out.

I wrote up a report of my visit for Father Raffin. In it I said that I thought the mother was almost certainly telling the truth.

How can you be so sure, given the boy hasn't uttered a word? he said.

I raised some objection, but finally yielded to his argument, which was that if we presented a weak case, Father Desbois was more likely to escape punishment.

I redrafted the end of my report, watered down my conclusion, and surmised that although the mother's accusations probably had some basis in fact, the boy had refused to comment. Raffin considered this a good outcome and gave the impression that he would personally follow up the report.

Several months went by before I heard anything, and then only by chance. I hadn't tried to contact Father Raffin, for I wished to be associated with him and with this affair as little as possible.

As it happened, I learned that the town had a new priest. Nothing was said about what had become of Father Desbois, and I didn't try to find out. However, I felt relieved and told myself that, despite everything, perhaps I had been of some use after all. Together with Father Raffin, whom I could not help but see in a new light.

A few weeks later, Sister Marie Agnès informed me that Father Raffin had been posted to the Vatican. She was thrilled; it wasn't every day that such an honor was bestowed upon a simple country priest. She spoke about the bright future that awaited him.

It was two years before I discovered that Father Desbois had simply been transferred—to Saint-Nazaire, to be precise. I felt betrayed, but obviously I had only myself to blame for I should have seen it coming. The church had closed ranks to protect itself. And my report had confirmed that it was impossible to establish the priest's guilt, and therefore futile to pursue the matter.

Páll had listened to my story in silence. The wind had risen and was buffeting Jesus, while the sea crashed onto the rocks before us.

You did everything you could, he said.

I looked out of the window.

And maybe the priest changed his ways.

No, I said. He didn't.

It was a sign of Páll's courtesy and intelligence that he didn't probe any further. Instead, he reversed out of the parking space, and we continued our journey along the shore.

I think we could do with a decent cup of coffee, he said. I haven't taken you to Mokka, yet. All the intellectuals go there. And the waffles are good, too.

THE LETTER HAD BEEN LYING DOWNSTAIRS ON THE mat inside the front door when one of the German nuns came home. She had picked it up and placed it on the kitchen table next to the sugar bowl and a little vase with a spray of dried grass.

The letter had been delivered by hand, and I instantly recognized the writing. Printed in blue ink on the envelope stood the words: Sister Johanna, 33 Ljósvallagata. I opened it.

You should speak with Jenný alone.

That was all. One line, and I was no closer to knowing the author's sex or age, no closer to knowing anything about him. Still, I examined each letter painstakingly and read the message over and over, as if it must yield some clue, compared it with the first letter, but was still in the dark.

Finally I set it aside, went over to the window, and looked out at the cemetery. It was getting dark. In the glow from a nearby streetlamp, I could see the outline of the freshly dug grave, a mound of earth which in time would become leveled, when the ground frost melted, the wreath on the mound. The words of the hymn echoed in my mind, dispersing my thoughts. I reached for a book of psalms I had found on the shelves in the living room. "The ways of the world all end in the same place . . ."

The coffee at Café Mokka had indeed been good and the waffles quite delicious. Páll's indifference to the stares people gave us when he shepherded me around the town continued to surprise me; he seemed utterly oblivious to them. Nor did he bat an eyelid when two young men, who as it turned out were friends of his, entered the café once we were sitting. He greeted them cheerfully and invited them to join us. They hesitated but then accepted, both courteous, rather shy to begin with and reluctant to say much.

Gústaf is a heathen—an Odinism follower, and Siggi is a devout atheist, said Páll, grinning, as he introduced us.

They looked slightly embarrassed, especially Siggi, but soon relaxed when I said:

More of an atheist than you, Páll?

I enjoyed their company. They were clever and funny, and when they saw me jotting down in my notebook words I hadn't heard before, they thought it a good idea to give me a few more.

Töffari, meaning "tough guy," said Siggi. Or *slappa af*, to chill, said Gústaf. That's more of a Danish expression, said Páll. Pedant, retorted Siggi.

They carried on in this vein, and I was happy to join in with their banter.

I've enjoyed meeting you intellectuals, I said, echoing Páll's words, as we rose from our seats.

We're not intellectuals. They're over by the door, said Gústaf, glancing at two rather sullen-looking types, speaking in hushed tones over their espressos.

Both friends of Páll, said Siggi.

At least one of them knew Páll, it turned out, because the man prodded him as we were leaving, and said:

Hey there, is that your new girlfriend?

I was halfway through the door but heard Páll's reply.

Yes, he said. We're engaged.

The thought made me smile, as I stood by the window looking out over the cemetery, then I collected myself, went back into the kitchen, and sat poring over the letter.

I was still sitting there an hour later when Páll rang the doorbell.

The handwriting is the same, he said. Who could it be?

Someone who is aware of all our comings and goings, I said.

We discussed whether this theory held up; Páll pointed out that the author would obviously assume that we'd interview the boys' parents, and that therefore the second letter was a logical continuation of the first. Possibly, I said. And yet I had the feeling that the author was following us closely.

Who else knows that we visited the couple? I said, thinking aloud.

Besides the bishop, said Páll, the couple themselves, the people they told, which includes Father August Frans, who doubtless complained of it to Miss Stein, and possibly a few of the teachers, who are close to him . . .

When three people know the whole nation knows, I said.

Páll had taught me this Icelandic saying the day before and smiled.

And of course I mentioned it to my mum and dad, he added.

We were scarcely any closer, and yet somehow our discussion had made it easier for me to think.

Jený, I said. What are we waiting for?

You, you mean, said Páll. The letter said alone, meaning one-on-one.

It was already five o'clock, so we decided to wait until the following morning, as Hermann would probably be on his way home from work. For my part, I was going to have a bowl of soup then attend evensong, which I was quite looking forward to that day. Páll planned to go to the cinema with a friend and was kind enough to ask me along. However, I declined, insisting that I was eager to go to bed early and read the book about Icelandic flora and soil reclamation I had found on the bookshelves.

I saw him to the door and was about to say good-bye and tell him I hoped he had a good time at the cinema, when he suddenly remembered something. He felt in his pocket, took out a piece of paper he had scribbled on, and handed it to me.

While I remember, I checked the national register before coming here. Halla Hjartardóttir is alive. She lives in Stykkishólmur on the Snæfellsnes Peninsula. Here's her address.

AFTER A LITTLE HESITATION, I TAKE THE PLUNGE and call Sister Marie Joseph. The sun is sinking in the sky, and the church casts its shadow all the way down the hill. I am still standing in the same spot in front of the Sacré-Coeur and have now decided that my visit has come to an end. It is time for me to get going to the airport, and besides I am convinced that there is no point in me stopping off at the guesthouse. I feel relieved after making that decision.

Before I left, Sister Marie Joseph offered to transfer my music from the iPod to my phone. But having both gadgets in one appeared too complicated, so I declined her offer. I don't know why I think of this now, as I tap in her number, perhaps it's just a sign of insecurity. She had already entered all my contacts, but when she showed me how to access them, I threw up my hands and asked her if she couldn't write instructions down for me on a piece of paper.

It's ringing, but I'm still not sure that I have dialed correctly. When she answers, I am so surprised that it is she who greets me.

Sister Johanna!

Good evening, I say, lowering my voice more than usual, in the hope that she will do the same.

It's Sister Johanna, I hear her say to the nuns in the room, then adding: I'm going outside.

Where are you now? she asks a moment later.

I tell her, then respond to her questions about the view, the acoustics in the church, and the organ, which she says she remembers so well.

When she asks if I have met anyone, I decide to tell her about the young couple who helped me with my suitcase, but not about those who have followed my every step and been in my thoughts all day. Those I keep to myself.

I am a little surprised that she doesn't ask me more about the young couple, but perhaps this isn't so strange. Instead she talks about my suitcase, fusses over me dragging it all around the city.

Aren't you exhausted?

I am certainly beginning to flag, but I try to play it down, insisting that the suitcase isn't heavy.

She says she noticed that when she took me to the station.

Do you think you took enough warm clothes with you?

It's summer, I remind her, and besides I'll have the use of a washing machine.

Then she says:

He has stopped howling. George Harrison. And he's got his appetite back. Do you want to hear him?

Heavens, no, I say. I shall only miss him even more.

He followed me to the rose garden today. Actually, he spent most of the time lying down by the wall next to the Pierre de Ronsard.

I take the opportunity to touch on a few things I feel I haven't emphasized enough.

Now that you mention it, I say, I may have forgotten to tell you that the roses on the north side of the garden don't need as much watering as the others, in particular the Amélie Gravereaux . . .

No, she says. You didn't forget.

She doesn't seem vexed, but I can tell from her voice that I should leave it there.

Well, then, I'll be on my way, I say.

Are you taking a taxi to the airport?

No, it's much too expensive, I say, commenting at the same time that I'm not sure about the best way to get to Gare du Nord.

Wait, she says, and I can hear her tapping on her phone. Take the metro at Barbès–Rochechouart, it's a ten-minute walk . . . Possibly a bit longer with the suitcase . . . Place Saint-Pierre to Rue Livingstone . . .

I tell her I know the way.

I think he knows that I'm talking to you.

What?

George Harrison. He just came over and is right beside me. I'm standing by the kitchen garden. He's gazing up at me, as if he knows I'm talking to you.

I find myself wishing that she hadn't said this, for now I feel a longing to go back. I can see George Harrison before me, his sad, melting eyes, the herb garden and the hedge dividing it from the house, the swallows that circle the buildings right before sundown, the fields that stretch all the way to the foot of the hills and the blue shroud that settles over them just before nightfall.

But I cannot go back. Not anymore.

I hurriedly say good-bye, put my phone in my pocket, and start down the hill. Ten minutes, she said, but now my night blindness has kicked in, or my fear of it at least. I walk slowly, taking care not to stumble, inching forward without looking back over my shoulder, not even when I have reached the bottom of the hill, even though with each step I feel my past behind me, those long-gone days boring into the back of my head, even as darkness envelops the streets.

ATTENDED EVENSONG, BUT MY MIND WAS ELSEWHERE.
Deus, in adjutorium meum intende, I chanted, with the same
passion as always, for the words certainly echoed what was in
my heart. *Domine, ad adjuvandum me festina*. I who believed
that I was coming to grips with myself and my assignment, I told
myself, I who believed that I would soon see land.

When I got back to Ljósvallagata, rather than go to bed with
my book on Icelandic flora and revegetation, I sat in the living
room with *Your Country, Iceland*—a five-volume series describing
the most noteworthy parts of the country in alphabetical order.
I had come across the collection in the bookshelves on my first
day there, and was slightly apprehensive, because I had noticed
that a couple of the volumes were missing. I was relieved then,
after a brief search, to find volume four, S–T, with a cover photo
of Arnarstapi, a small fishing village on the southern side of the
Snæfellsnes Peninsula.

But it was Stykkishólmur I was after, on the northern side. It
didn't take me long to find it and, while the article was short and
rather dry, I quickly lost myself in it.

First, I looked at the photographs, two of them taken from
the air, one from the harbor. A small coastal village with a few

islands out to sea, mountains with snowy peaks on the far side of the fjord. Summer. The sea was blue and calm, the white houses had red and green roofs, and everything was so still and bright, and yet so alien. Perhaps it was the time of year, the sun shining on the village, making the colors so vibrant and cheerful that I felt as if I had seen everything in monochrome since I arrived in the country.

The German nuns retired to bed early, and I sat alone in the living room for a long time poring over the book. There were only two or three pages of text, most of it easy for me to understand, although occasionally I had to consult the dictionary, and by the time I got up to go to bed, I could remember most of it by heart.

"Stykkishólmur is the biggest town on the Snæfellsnes Peninsula. Population 1,242 on December 1, 1982 . . . It has a shipyard . . . A construction business . . . Three timber merchants and wood workshops . . . Fish liver, shellfish, and shrimp processing plants, a saltfish factory. A primary school, a music school, a brass band, choirs. It has the oldest weather station in the country. And a telephone exchange."

The letters Halla wrote to me when she arrived back in Iceland showed how fluent she had become in French. In her early letters, she recalled various things that had happened that winter, said many wonderful things about our time together, was occasionally funny, but also talked about how empty the room had felt after I moved out. She wanted to hear my news, and said that she hoped I was well, that I was happy. Those were her words. That I was happy.

She signed off with *Je t'embrasse* and told me she missed me. I thought about our final embrace the morning she left, the orange scarf about her neck, the green Citroën driving off.

When at last I replied, I felt as if Raffin were standing over me, reading every word I wrote. The result was so bland and formal that I didn't expect ever to hear from her again. But she did write back, shortly after starting her studies at the University of Iceland, and she asked me if something was the matter. I didn't answer.

No, I never answered.

I always intended to, and when I moved from Sacré-Coeur to the little convent in the nineteenth arrondissement, I took her letters with me and sat down more than once with paper and pen at the tiny writing desk in my cell. But in the end I gave up, because I could neither reveal my thoughts to her nor bring myself to humiliate her by writing yet another empty, dishonest letter.

She will soon forget me, I told myself, *when her life takes off in Iceland, she will have plenty of other things to think about.* And it seems that was the case, for I never heard from her again.

There were a few small boats in the photographs of the harbor, as well as some bigger ships and a ferry which they said delivered the post to the islands in Breiðafjörður and made scheduled stop-offs in the Westfjords. But what most interested me were the houses in the town, as I tried to imagine where she might live. I found a map of Stykkishólmur at the back of the telephone directory, and compared it to the photographs, but as the only one showing the entire town was taken from a distance, it was of little use.

Even so, I tried to imagine her in these pictures. Emerging from one of the houses—a white one with a green gable roof—closing the door behind her, and then the gate, walking down the street, turning right toward the harbor. But I couldn't think why she would be going there, and soon I lost sight of her and had difficulty conjuring her again. The town was so strange and empty.

There were no people in the photographs. No sign of life. One might be forgiven for thinking it was a ghost town.

One sentence stayed with me longer than any other. I don't know why, and of course it would be foolish of me to make too much out of it: "In 1936 a hospital was founded by the Franciscan order, which has since been run by Franciscan nuns, who established a convent in Stykkishólmur."

No, it was absurd to try to connect Halla's life in Stykkishólmur to the nuns, even more absurd to imagine any association between their existence and mine. But my mind was in turmoil, my feelings all over the place. I only realized this afterward, but by then it was too late.

Just after midnight, I closed the book and returned the telephone directory to the hallway. It was windy outside, and after getting into bed, I listened for a long time to the snow lashing the windows, until finally I managed to fall asleep.

PÁLL ARRIVED JUST AFTER NINE THE NEXT DAY. FROM the living room window, I watched him negotiate with difficulty a mound of snow as he tried to park Jesus across the street. I had skipped midmorning mass and hadn't bothered to excuse myself to the German nuns, who didn't try to conceal their disapproval at my absence.

When he came in, he explained that he had just come from Bergstaðastræti, where he had seen Hermann Atlason drive off in his car. Normally, I would have praised his resourcefulness, but my mind was elsewhere. I felt tense and was having trouble concentrating; for example, I spent ages searching for my coat, which was staring at me from the closet in the hallway.

Páll must have sensed that I wasn't quite myself, because when we were in the car, he asked if I'd slept badly.

It was windy last night, I said, and there were snowstorms.

I didn't notice, he said, grinning, doubtless hoping I would follow his example and lighten up. But I was thinking about Stykkishólmur and its deserted streets, the front gardens where no tree or shrub grew. Loneliness. Emptiness. Both for her and me.

All at once, everything seemed upside down, my assignment utterly futile, my life equally so.

How long does it take to drive to Stykkishólmur? I asked suddenly as we stopped at a red light.

What?

To Stykkishólmur. How long?

It depends on the roads. In summer, it takes about three hours, I think.

The pavement outside had been cleared, as had the path to the house. Páll said he would wait down the street, adding that Jenný might get nervous if she knew he was there. I nodded, as I climbed out of the car.

She looked worried as soon as she opened the door.

Sister Johanna, she said, then added: My husband isn't here.

May I come in?

She hesitated then opened the door wider and stood aside.

I followed her silently into the living room and sat on the sofa beneath the portrait of our Savior. She sat opposite me and waited for me to speak. If I hadn't been in such a state, I would have started on a casual note, discussing the weather or the latest news of the pope, who had been rushed to the hospital with acute appendicitis the day before, but was recovering well according to reports in the media. However, I was much too agitated for that and found it difficult enough simply concentrating on my reason for being there.

I am here because of your son.

I could see that she already knew this. Even so, she gave a start, quickly averting her eyes, and said nothing. I reached into my bag, took out the letter, and was going to hand it to her, but then fortunately thought better of it. Later, when I came to my senses, I felt dizzy at the thought that not only had I been about to show her how little evidence we had, but also to inform her about Jón Karlsson and the accusations of indecent conduct made on his behalf.

She looked at the letter in my hand.

What has your son said to you about Father August Frans?

She turned pale, wiped her forehead, her gaze sliding, as though unintentionally, toward the image of the Savior behind me on the wall.

My husband . . . I must call him.

And yet she didn't stand up, but rather watched as I put on my glasses and unfolded the letter.

There was no need for me to do so because I knew the words by heart. But I did anyway, reading with great effort the parts which I knew would remain forever etched on her memory.

She sat motionless. Normally, my heart would have bled for her, but that morning I wasn't myself.

I wanted to leave. I wanted to end this conversation as soon as possible, to end this assignment, to get away from this filth. I had to see Halla. I had to go to Stykkishólmur. I could think of nothing else.

You are aware of this, I said.

He didn't describe it in those words . . . he's just a child . . . I don't believe it. . . .

She had started to sob.

But you are aware of it.

No, I . . . I can't . . .

I should have held her in my arms, said I would help her, spoken of forgiveness and love, declared that we would stand together. But it didn't enter my head, for charity wasn't uppermost in my mind. On the contrary, I was filled with rage, disgust, a longing to bring matters to a head. Get away. I wanted to get away.

What did he say had happened?

She slowly found her tongue but had difficulty getting the words out, stopping and starting, speaking falteringly. In brief, she finally managed to tell me that her son was afraid of the headmaster and of Miss Stein and had told her that they hurt him.

They hurt him?

Yes, she said.

How?

He didn't say.

Did you ask?

No . . . I couldn't. I asked my husband to talk to him.

She started sobbing again.

It was a mistake. I should have known that Kristján would be evasive.

Why?

They are so different, father and son. Although Hermann is very fond of the boy, of course . . .

The winter sun was climbing in the sky and cast a faint light on the leafless trees outside the window. A plastic bag had gotten caught on one of the branches. Every now and then, the wind would shake it.

Hermann spoke to Father August Frans, she continued. He said he had been forced to discipline Kristján. He said that if he wanted to get on in life he had to learn to focus. Hermann believed him and gave Kristján a talking-to.

What did you do?

She rubbed her eyes.

Nothing. I . . .

I was impatient and rose from my chair. The woman hesitated, and I had the impression that she was going to say something else. But she waited until we were in the hallway when I was about to leave.

One evening when he was in bed . . .

I turned around.

. . . he said to me: Mummy, they touched me, they touched me, Mummy.

She was in tears when I left.

I SHOULD HAVE KNOWN MY VISIT TO BERGSTAÐASTRÆTI would have consequences. It wasn't difficult to imagine the ensuing conversation between Jenný and her husband, and his response was predictable. Perhaps she had tried standing up to him, found the necessary strength, before finally backing down, as I suspected she had always done.

Before the day was out, I had been summoned to see Bishop Johnson. Páll and I had driven straight from Bergstaðastræti to Vesturgata, changed our mind about stopping off at Mokka, as Páll had suggested earlier, although clearly he was still longing for a good cup of coffee. But I was fired up and wanted to get to Karólína Símonardóttir's as soon as possible. We parked in the same spot as before and walked back along the road toward her house, for the sidewalk was still covered in snow and ice.

I planned to read to her from the letter and demand a response. But she didn't come to the door, and after knocking a few times, Páll looked at me and shook his head. I was convinced that she was home, had seen us approach or heard us talking, and I told him so.

What can we do? he asked, and we left it at that.

I felt I had been abrupt with Páll, who deserved better, so I suggested we now go to Mokka, as we had nothing else to do for the moment. Once we were sitting with our coffee and waffles, I relayed my conversation with Jený, which until then I had been too upset to share with him.

Is that what she said? he asked, unable to conceal his shock.

Are you surprised?

He didn't answer.

I was relieved that none of his friends were among the other customers this time. We munched our waffles in silence, watching the people come and go. We reordered two espressos. I could tell that he was upset.

He had to stop by the office, so I took the opportunity to attend lunchtime prayers at the church. My mind was still in turmoil, and my conversation with God didn't last long. When I left, Páll was waiting for me on the steps outside.

The bishop wants to see you, he said. He's on pins and needles.

I followed him silently to the bishop's office. The wind had picked up and was blowing powdery snow across the lawn around the church. I had meant to buy a more sensible pair of shoes when I arrived, but hadn't done so yet, and now I regretted it.

No sooner had we walked through the door than Hildur, the bishop's secretary, told us to go straight into his office. I took off my coat and hung it up before following Páll. Hildur watched me, looking down at her typewriter when I turned toward her, her face as inscrutable as always.

Bishop Johnson was standing in the middle of the room, and I guessed that he had been watching us as we walked across the lawn. He seemed taller than before, but also more stooped, almost hunched over in fact.

Sister Johanna, what have you done?

I waited for him to continue.

I received a call from Hermann Atlason. His wife is dreadfully upset after your visit—if one can call it that.

I beg your pardon?

He says you didn't even announce your visit, but simply barged in.

And you believe that?

What did you say to her exactly?

I read her part of the letter you forwarded to the Vatican.

His look of bewilderment was nothing less than pitiful.

The contents didn't surprise her, I added.

He sat down at the coffee table while I remained standing and gave an account of my conversation with Jený. He listened in silence, eyes fixed straight ahead, as if he were thinking of something else. He didn't look up when I had finished but said in a hushed voice: Did you prohibit her from calling her husband?

If you believe that, perhaps you should speak with her yourself, I said.

Had he not understood where my inquiry might lead, or had his hopes that I would fail clouded his judgment?

I don't believe it, the bishop suddenly blurted, and I had no doubt that he was sincere.

I didn't dislike him, despite his feebleness and disinclination toward action. I knew the type: a bibliophile who joined the church to devote himself entirely to study and had little need to concern himself with worldly affairs. Sacrificing the desires of the flesh in exchange for a life of letters would have posed little difficulty for him. He was scarcely orthodox, but respected tradition, and doubtless approved of the church's moral message, while placing books and studies above everything else. Affairs of this nature were anathema to him; they turned his rarefied world upside down and made a mess of the life he had constructed for himself.

As I watched him in deep thought, chin resting on his hand, I imagined that he was conversing with God (politely, of course) about the predicament he found himself in. He had never sought high office, was content with this diocese at the ends of the earth, which few considered enviable, for it allowed him to pursue his interests in peace and quiet—in a place where nothing could disturb his serenity, least of all the few Catholics who lived there. And then this . . .

No, I did not dislike Bishop Johnson, yet I had no sympathy for him either. Perhaps he understood this from my silence.

What happens next? he said at last, and I thought it as likely that he was posing the question to God as well as me.

We wait, I said.

Hermann threatened to call Father August Frans.

I did not reply.

I begged him for goodness' sake to let it rest.

Páll has been listening quietly throughout, and I almost gave a start when he opened his mouth, not least because of his solemn tone.

Does Hermann not understand what his son said to his mother?

The bishop looked at him, but apparently didn't know the answer or lacked the will to articulate it. For my part, I wanted to bring the conversation to an end.

We can't be sure that she told him, I said to Páll. And we can't trust her to repeat it.

At last, Bishop Johnson rose from his chair, when I started toward the door.

Sister Johanna, tread carefully. I shall pray for these people. Perhaps you should do the same.

Half a gale was blowing outside, and I had the impression that it was snowing, although with the wind it was difficult to tell. I could barely walk straight, and before I knew it, Páll's arm was looped through mine.

I need to buy winter boots, I said.

I'll ask my mom about shops, he said.

Jesus was waiting for us on a side street. I helped Páll scrape the windows, and once we were inside, after he had started the engine, we both rubbed our hands.

How can we find out whether the road to Stykkishólmur is clear? I asked as we drove off.

SISTER MARIE JOSEPH SENDS ME A PHOTOGRAPH OF George Harrison when I am on the train to the airport. I know she means well, but still I feel a pang in my heart, to use her turn of phrase, and I immediately try to think of a reason to turn back. He is standing by the kitchen door gazing up at her, with such a sorrowful expression that I feel close to tears. But more than anything it is her message that makes me feel that way, as it explains the picture: "He has started looking for you all over the place again. He wants to go on his evening walk."

This is the exact time, after supper and evening prayers, when everything has quieted down and the light is fading. Our usual route takes us through the rose garden, where we inspect the day's work—discuss what needs to be done the next morning and bid our friends good night—then alongside the kitchen garden, through the vineyard and out into the fields that roll westward, turning blue as night falls. Often, we continue toward the foothills that divide the grounds of the convent from the nearest farm, for George Harrison is in no hurry to return and does everything he can to lead me on, sometimes beyond dusk. But we know the way so well we could walk home blindfolded, even in winter when it gets dark early.

However, I cannot go back now, and I return the phone to my

pocket, no longer able to bear the look in George Harrison's eyes. I also refrain from asking Sister Marie Joseph if she isn't intending to take him for a walk, as I fear she will tire of my meddling if I'm not careful.

I have no choice but to look at the report, which I've been carrying with me halfway around the city. Maybe I'll get to it on the plane. Or when I have checked in, assuming I can find a comfortable seat at the airport where I won't be disturbed. Raffin seemed adamant that I reread it. Unnecessarily so, I thought, but perhaps that was just my imagination.

Two years ago, I heard he was struggling with ill health. Sister Marie Agnès told me about it, but was unable to provide any details, although she understood that it was serious, and he perhaps was even near death's door. She had a doleful look on her face when she summoned me to break the news, for she had always been under the impression that the cardinal and I were close. He had never told her the facts, not out of consideration toward me, but because of course his power is based upon knowing what others don't.

But anyway, the man was unwell. Sister Marie Agnès offered to pray for him with me. And so, I was forced to kneel with her in the chapel every day, even though I would almost have preferred to think about anything else other than the cardinal.

It is not difficult to show kindness to those we love, or even to strangers who might be in distress; it is easy to show relative consideration. The real test comes when we must forgive those who have done us harm, show love to our enemy. It is a test of our faith, our strength of mind. I tried, I dug as deep into my soul as I could, deeper even than I intended, but I was clutching at air.

It shames me to admit that I hoped he would find peace. Or

rather, that I would find peace from him. Even so, I battled with these thoughts, looked to the cross for strength, or at Sister Marie Agnès beside me, head bowed, hands clasped in perfect meditation. But to no avail. I hoped he would die.

I have scarcely seen Sister Marie Agnès as cheerful as when she heard that our prayers had been answered, as she put it. I recall that I was harvesting vegetables with some of the other nuns when we saw her approach; she was walking as fast as her legs would carry her, and her excitement was obvious, even from a distance. I suspected instantly that she brought news of the cardinal, and my heart sank when she called out my name for the first time, having only reached the toolshed: "Sister Johanna, Sister Johanna!" for it was clear from her voice that the news was good.

At the supper table, she announced the tidings to all the other nuns, though many of them didn't even know who Cardinal Raffin was, declaring that his recovery was proof of God's love. Her eyes sought out mine, and she beamed at me, and I tried to smile back. God's love. *Gloria Patri, et Filio, et Spiritui Sancto.*

We have nearly reached the airport. It is eight thirty. I double-check that I have my ticket and passport, before getting up and walking over to the doors. Perhaps I was hoping deep down that I had forgotten my passport; in any event, I wasn't relieved to find that I hadn't.

Four days. That's all, I tell myself. Four days. This time around Raffin and I agreed that my visit should be as brief as possible.

PÁLL ACCOMPANIED ME TO A SHOP DOWNTOWN WHERE I bought a pair of winter boots. It was a warm and comfortable store, and the sales assistants, all middle-aged women, were extremely helpful. In a fanciful moment, I thought I might buy myself a skirt suit, or even a dress—there was one in particular, a black one, which I had seen on a mannequin in the window. I joked about it with Páll while I was trying on different shoes. He was clearly relieved to see that I was my old self again and asked whether it wouldn't be a better idea for me to buy something red or blue, for a change. At first, the woman serving us didn't know what to make of our banter, but then she broke into a smile.

That was the morning after our meeting with Bishop Johnson. Nothing new had happened since then, except that the previous evening we had knocked once more on the door of Jón Karlsson and his mother, but to no avail. The house was dark, but a lady who lived across the street and had clearly been watching us called out her window:

She's not there. Then added: Thank God. We tried to engage her, but desisted when she closed the window and drew the curtain.

My new boots were warm, calf-length, lined with fur, soft. The sales assistant told me she herself had a pair and enthused about them. They were Swedish, she said, as she showed me how well made they were.

And reasonably priced, she added.

I only mentioned Stykkishólmur when we were back in the car and had agreed that all we could do was wait. Páll said he would try to find out if Jón Karlsson had turned up at school that morning; he told me that before picking me up at half past nine to go shoe shopping, he had driven past the house on Vesturgata but not seen anybody there. I encouraged him, then brought up my idea—as if it had occurred to me in the same breath.

Stykkishólmur. On your own?

I told Páll that I had called the highway authorities that morning, on the advice of my neighborhood grocer, with whom I had become friendly. Páll looked rather sheepish and muttered something about how he should have already done that for me.

Nonsense, I said. I must be able to do some things for myself.

I'll go with you if you want.

That's absolutely unnecessary. Do you think you can survive without Jesus for a day?

Páll was visibly concerned when we switched seats. But Jesus was easy to drive, and he calmed down when he realized I had no difficulty changing gears or turning right or left, despite the somewhat heavy steering.

Have you checked the weather forecast? he said. You can never be sure here in Iceland.

I confessed I hadn't thought of that, and he turned on the radio, as the forecast was due any moment. We listened closely and discovered that the weather was supposed to be calm until later that night, when the north wind would start to pick up.

When do you plan to leave?

As soon as possible, I said.

It'll probably be dark when you drive back, he said.

I told him I realized that.

Unless you stay the night . . .

I told him that was unlikely.

It's a three-hour journey, at least.

I nodded.

Hvalfjörður takes forever to drive around.

I had to stop off at Ljósvallagata to pick up some warmer clothes, and Páll accompanied me, said he could walk from there up to Landakot. I was touched by his concern, but I couldn't wait for him to leave.

So it *was* her? he said, when I had parked without any trouble farther down the street.

I was a bit startled, but tried not to let it show, and simply nodded.

You found her number?

Yes, I said, and changed the subject, asking him about the mileage and whether I should buy petrol before I left town, or on the way there. He suggested I fill the tank in the town of Borgarnes, about an hour from Reykjavík, which would get me to Stykkishólmur and back.

Are you sure you don't want me to come with you? I can wait outside in the car while you visit her. Or just walk around the town.

Again, I said no, told him not to worry about me, then I locked the car and put the key in my bag.

Inside, he showed me a road map he had taken from the glove compartment. The route seemed fairly straightforward to me, but he insisted I keep my eyes open.

And drive carefully, there could still be ice on the roads even if they have been cleared, he added.

He watched as I drove off. It was eleven o'clock. When I turned the corner, I thought I saw a glimmer of sunshine in the rearview mirror.

THE FORECAST WAS ACCURATE FOR THE FIRST LEG of my journey. The glimmer of sunshine became a pale wintry light, and Jesus and I had no trouble finding our way out of town and onto the highway. There wasn't much traffic, mainly trucks, and it comforted me to know they were there, even though I wasn't worried at all about getting lost or running into problems.

I tried to enjoy the views, and to begin with I succeeded. As soon as I left the suburbs, I was greeted by mountains, snow-covered meadows stretching down to the shore, farmhouses dotted here and there, fjords and coves. The landscape was truly stunning, but equally daunting, and as I approached Hvalfjörður I started to feel a creeping sense of unease.

It actually began as I was driving along Mount Esja, when all of a sudden the wind started shaking the car, but it wasn't until I reached Hvalfjörður that it really got to me. By then the sun had disappeared behind the clouds, and the light I had been enjoying gave way to a grayness that seemed to come as much from the peaks of the surrounding mountains as up from the fjord itself. For some time, Jesus and I had been alone on the road with no vehicle ahead of us or in the rearview mirror, and that spooked me, strange though it may sound. I instinctively stepped on the gas, keen to get out of that never-ending fjord as quickly as possible, but realized my mistake at the first bend when the car started sliding on the icy road. I lost control and might easily have ended up in a cold ditch if the tires hadn't suddenly caught traction on the gravel underneath.

I dared not stop, but immediately slowed down, inching forward until my heart stopped pounding. It dawned on me that it wasn't the mountains I was afraid of, or the deep, black waters of the fjord, or even the grayness that had swooped down on me, but rather my own inner landscape, the darkness that lurked there, the abyss.

What was I expecting from this trip? I couldn't answer that question, and by the time I pulled over at the Ferstikla service stop, I felt exhausted. I considered turning back, which of course is what I should have done, but I guess I didn't have the energy. It was probably less bother to press on, and so, after having a coffee and resting for a while, Jesus and I continued on our way out of the fjord.

The remainder of the journey was uneventful. I didn't think about the views, or what awaited me. Instead, I concentrated on driving, and sure enough, after Borgarnes, the wind started to rise again. The plows hadn't done such a good job clearing the snow as they had closer to Reykjavík, and soon the road seemed to merge with the white landscape. I drove along at a snail's pace, but when I reached Mýrar, I was fortunate enough to find myself behind a delivery truck. I had no difficulty keeping pace with it, and thus I kept going as the winter sun appeared occasionally over the sea to the west and shone for a while on the road and the surrounding fields.

I had taken out volume four of *Your Country, Iceland*, but left it on the kitchen table at Ljósvallagata. It came to me as I drove into the town, and for an instant I felt as if I had made a huge blunder, but then I realized that I knew the chapter on Stykkishól-mur by heart, and I calmed down. However, now that I was there, the place looked completely alien to me, probably because all I had seen were aerial photographs taken on a bright, summer's day. I slowed to a halt to get my bearings.

My fears proved unfounded, for it was almost impossible to get lost in Stykkishólmur. Even so, I hesitated, driving slowly along the roads at the edge of town; Neskinn, I read on one sign, Áskinn on another, before driving down a dead-end street and turning around. Finally, I headed for the harbor, past a garage and a fishnet factory, the school, and a car wash, crawling along, for I had no idea what I proposed to do when I arrived at 23 Thórsgata.

I didn't see a soul until I reached the harbor. I pulled over outside a little shop, but stayed in the car. A forklift and some trucks drove around on the quayside, a small boat came in to land, and two children were riding up and down on their bicycles, amusing themselves by letting the wheels skid where the ground was icy. Otherwise, nothing happened, and of course I saw no sign of Halla.

I couldn't imagine her in this place. It had been difficult enough at the kitchen table in Ljósvallagata examining the photographs in the book, but now, as I sat in the car, I found it almost impossible to understand why she had decided to spend her life here. I had always pictured her in bright sunlight, surrounded by people. Not that I could conjure the faces of those around her, but I could sense their presence, their warmth, because she was forever smiling in my mind, as if she was having amusing conversations or thinking funny thoughts. Her elegant movements, her slender shoulders, her fingers as she tucked her hair behind her ears, did not belong in such a place. Not that dreamy mind that got lost in thought at the slightest provocation, not that lover of beauty, who could stand outside a shop window in the Latin Quarter and marvel over the way some small objects, which I hardly noticed, were displayed.

There was a handwritten notice about opening times in the shop window and, on the windowsill, a container of soap which someone must have left when they were cleaning, although not recently, as dust and some dirt were noticeable when I walked in. The woman who greeted me asked immediately if I was new. I begged her pardon, then realized that of course the townsfolk were used to seeing the nuns at the convent, so I explained that I was visiting and ordered a coffee from a machine behind the counter.

It was watery and didn't taste of much, but I drank it all the same, and ate a twist donut to keep me going. I didn't stay long, and when I left the sky was clouding over.

I drove up to Thórsgata. I hadn't needed to take the telephone directory with me when I left Reykjavík, for I knew the street names by heart. Indeed, I've always had a good sense of direction and find it easy to memorize the way to places. I was no nearer to having a plan and was growing more and more anxious, yet at the same time I desperately longed to see her.

Far from being white with a green gable roof, the house was a gray bungalow with a blue roof. Newly built, I thought, with an adjoining garage, in front of which was parked a small, white Japanese car. I drove past without stopping, accelerating rather than slowing down, because, all at once, I felt as if I was doing something wrong. Then I turned around, and this time I drove past slowly to get a better view of her house.

There was a light in the window between the front door and the garage: the kitchen, I assumed. But I couldn't see anyone, and not wanting to idle in the middle of the road, I turned around again and parked a little down the street, from where I was able to watch the house.

Once, when Halla was helping me with my Icelandic, I remember struggling with the word *fallegt*. I had just learned the definition of *fall*, meaning "to fall" or "to drop," and was trying to make a connection but getting completely lost. The sentence, as I recall, was *blómið er fallegt*, meaning "the flower is beautiful," and I imagined petals falling in winter or something like that. She shook her head, forbidding me to look in the dictionary, because she insisted the word had come up before and I ought to know it by now. I was being unusually slow that day, so she tried to give me a few hints, all of which I have forgotten, save the last: *Það er svo fallegt að horfa á þig hugsa*—it's beautiful watching you when you are thinking.

Those were her exact words. I remember, because I wrote them down with her help, together with a few other pointers. But it was the look in her eyes that made me understand the meaning of the word, the look in her eyes, and the silence that followed. I was on the verge of saying something I might have regretted, but fortunately I hesitated just long enough for her to grin in a way that made me realize she was simply making fun of my obtuseness.

I sat in the car for close to a half hour without seeing any movement in or around the house. In the meantime, a car drove past and pulled up outside a warehouse down the road. A man got out, fetched a box from the facility, and then drove off. Nothing else happened.

It had started to get dark when a jeep drove up to the house and parked outside the garage. I gave a start, as I saw the driver get out, a middle-aged man with blond hair. He opened the trunk and took out two shopping bags. Seconds later the passenger stepped out, but as she was hidden from view, I didn't see her until she walked behind the car.

She was facing me directly, and for a moment I had the impression that she was looking straight at me. I leaned forward, half crying out her name, and was about to open the door and clamber out when I stopped myself.

I watched her go into the house. The door closed, and a moment later, lights went on in a couple of windows. I felt drained, barely able to move. I looked at the house, the car, the lights, and waited for the shock to pass. I realized I would never leave the car and knock on the door, and yet I couldn't tear myself away, clinging to the image I had of her facing me.

Thirty yards away, perhaps less.

Darkness fell. The clouds thickened. Then it began to snow.

PÁLL WOKE ME. IT WAS NEARLY TEN O'CLOCK. I WAS so exhausted after the trip that I hadn't heard the German nuns that morning.

Are you not feeling well? he asked, when I opened the door.

I told him I had arrived home late.

Something happened, he said.

I was in my nightgown and asked him to wait in the kitchen while I got dressed. It took me quite a long time, for my mind was still in turmoil and my body felt stiff. By the time I joined him, he had made tea and put bread and cheese on the table.

He would undoubtedly have asked about my trip had he not been so preoccupied. I had barely sat down and poured myself a cup of tea when he started telling me his story. To begin with I had difficulty following him, which was unusual.

The evening before, he was leaving the cinema with a friend (a woman friend, he clarified later), when it occurred to him to take a detour via Vesturgata. They were walking, and when they reached the corner, they saw there was a party at Jón Karlsson's mother's house—a jolly one, to put it mildly. The front door was wide open with some guests lingering outside as music and singing blared from within. They paused for a moment, but since people seemed to be coming and going freely, they decided to go inside.

The living room was packed, with more men than women. Karólína was standing by the piano singing, although by the sound of it both she and her accompanist were well in their cups. The same applied to most if not all the guests, some of whom sang along, although the majority seemed more interested in drinking.

Páll said that Karólína hadn't recognized him, or indeed even noticed him and his friend. Unsurprisingly, he added, as she certainly didn't seem to keep a guest list of any sort. She was all dressed up, in a red gown with a fur collar, her hair loose. A middle-aged man encouraged the guests to give regular bursts of applause to show their appreciation, sometimes in the middle of a song, and Karólína was clearly lapping up the attention.

I don't know where she thought she was, Páll said. She seemed completely in a world of her own.

They had wandered into the kitchen, where people were mixing drinks with the associated din. Nobody took any notice of them, and, leaving his friend there, Páll had discreetly made his way to the bedrooms.

The door to Karólína's was ajar. Everything was upside down, clothes strewn over the unmade bed and on the floor, wardrobe doors flung open. But the door to her son's bedroom was closed. Páll said that he had paused for a moment then turned the handle. The door was locked. He considered announcing himself, but didn't.

Karólína was taking a break, and Páll found her in the kitchen when he came back. She stared at him for a moment, as though trying to place him. But she soon gave up, and it was only when he introduced himself that she remembered him.

She was startled.

What are you doing here?

I happened to be walking by.

I'm giving a little concert.

Páll said that he could see that.

Where is your son?

She didn't reply immediately, but glanced toward the bedrooms.

He's asleep. I always make sure he goes to bed early and does his homework. Just like I told Father August Frans.

Have you spoken to him recently?

Yesterday. I spoke to him yesterday. And that nun you came here with had better leave my Jón alone.

She raised her voice.

You can tell her that from me, she said. If some foreigners start meddling, then Father August Frans won't be able to help him, he'll have to let him go.

Is that what he told you?

She didn't reply.

I always put Jón to bed when I give my little concerts.

At that moment, the man who had been encouraging people to show their appreciation for her singing walked in.

Lína, my dear, they are waiting for you. More songs! Let me kiss you . . .

Páll thought she would doubtless have acquiesced had he not been standing right next to her.

I think you should leave, she said. I didn't invite you.

And so, of course, we did, said Páll. What else could we do?

I poured myself another cup of tea, and we gazed out the kitchen window at the snow wafting gently to the ground.

Páll's story didn't surprise me, but I was still too numb to say so, or indeed to make any useful comments. My mind remained in the west, in the twilight on Thórsgata. I had stepped out of the car and was standing hidden from view across the street, where I could see her in the kitchen, first alone at the stove, then with her husband as they sat down to eat. It was snowing, and I was trying to imagine what they might be saying to each other, although mostly I was just staring at her profile, waiting for her to smile. She didn't, and when at last I drove away, I felt as if something had been lost to me forever.

Páll also remained silent, but I wasn't so blind that I couldn't see that he was biting his tongue.

I went back there this morning, he said at last, looking rather sheepish. I know you said we shouldn't talk to the boys without their parents, but . . .

Where did you go?

I went back to Vesturgata. I couldn't stop thinking about the boy locked in his bedroom. I arrived at half past seven. About a quarter of an hour later he appeared—school starts at eight. I followed him, but only called out to him when we were away from the house.

Obviously, I did my best not to scare him off, but he was clearly nervous and wouldn't reply. As I got closer, he snapped at me, told me to go away. Then he ran off.

Páll fell silent.

I realize this was a mistake, he said after a while. I'm sorry.

I mustered a smile of encouragement. I knew the feeling; I understood his anger and helplessness. I remembered as if it were yesterday the expression on the face of the mother whose son Father Desbois had abused. Except that I had backed down. I had provided Cardinal Raffin with a way out. Páll didn't seem willing to do that.

Jesus is aptly named, I said.

Páll asked me what I meant.

I set off far too late yesterday evening from Stykkishólmur. It had started to snow. The car got stuck and I didn't know what to do. There was nobody around, no traffic at all. I sat there for over an hour and was ready to give up when all of a sudden we lurched forward. It was a miracle. Your friends hit the nail on the head when they gave him that name.

As I might have expected, Páll took advantage of my story to scold my recklessness, recalling his numerous offers to accompany me to Stykkishólmur. That had also been my intention, for he stopped expostulating about his own blunders and focused instead on mine. I didn't protest or try to make excuses, but simply nodded in silence, until he said: I don't understand how your friend could have let you leave. Obviously, you should have stayed the night with her.

Then I jumped to her defense, muttering something about how I was the only one to blame.

I MANAGE TO FIND A SEAT BY THE WINDOW, WITH A VIEW over the tarmac and at least one of the runways. My flight has been delayed; departure is now in an hour and a half. I am comfortable, and there aren't too many other passengers here at the gate. I imagine they have taken the opportunity to shop or get some refreshments.

At last I have opened the report and am flicking through it. Nothing in it comes as a surprise to me, although I realize that I clearly focused on the main points and left out some details. But I do mention our visit with Bishop Johnson the day after my trip to Stykkishólmur, at midday to be exact, when Páll and I had stood up from the kitchen table at Ljósvallagata, having discussed our respective blunders and the fact that we were at a loss as to what we ought to be doing next.

The bishop was less than happy to see us, although obviously he tried not to let it show. We told him about Páll's visit to Vesturgata the previous evening, but omitted to mention his attempt that morning to speak with Jón Karlsson. The bishop listened in silence, only responding when I made my request.

You can't talk to the teachers behind Father August Frans's back!

I'd like to start with Miss Stein.

That's out of the question!

In which case you must speak to him about it.

And what shall I say, Sister Johanna? What shall I say?

I explained to him that Father August Frans almost certainly knew about the letter, that Jený had undoubtedly told her husband about it, and that he had informed the headmaster. In which case it was best to be blunt with him. There was no reason to wait.

He also knows about our visit to Karólína Símonardóttir. That much became clear last night.

The bishop shook his head.

I wasn't expecting things to blow up like this. Cardinal Raffin maintained that . . .

He fell silent. I waited for him to go on.

I don't like it, he said presently. I don't like it at all. You're playing with fire, Sister Johanna.

I reminded him of what Jený had told me, and the situation at Jón Karlsson's house, Karólína Símonardóttir's confirmation that Father August Frans had tried to silence her and her son.

Were those her words?

In some sense, I replied.

Didn't you say she was drunk? he asked, turning to Páll. How then are we to take her seriously?

He finally yielded, or rather he ended the conversation, declaring that he needed peace and quiet to be able to think the matter over.

I can talk to him myself if you prefer, I said, before we left, but the bishop simply shook his head.

When we stepped outside, we saw Father August Frans in the distance, on his way from the school to the church. Despite the fact that it was snowing and the temperature had dropped well below freezing, he hadn't bothered to put on an overcoat. I noticed he had a slight limp and asked Páll about it.

He has always limped. He manages to hide it, except when he has to walk longer distances. He doesn't like people to talk about it.

Why? I asked.

He shrugged.

Who knows? He's vain.

Instead of walking along Túngata, and from there up the steps to the church, he was making a beeline across the lawn toward the door. From the way he was striding, he seemed in a bad mood, or that's what I said to Páll.

It's quite possible, he replied. There's been a problem with the church bells recently. That's probably why he's going there.

We watched the headmaster disappear into the church. Páll explained to me that the bells were from Holland, as was Father August Frans himself, and so it had somehow become his responsibility to deal with the manufacturers whenever there was an issue.

All of a sudden, last week, they started to toll by themselves, said Páll. The priest and the deacon checked the control panel, which appeared to be in order. So they called Father August Frans. Clearly, he hasn't gotten to the bottom of it either, and I expect that annoys him. He's terribly proud of his knowledge of the bells and won't let anyone else near them.

We stood for a while, expecting them to start ringing at any moment, but when that didn't happen, we walked off.

I had been about to knock on the door the evening before. As I stood watching her prepare the supper from across the street, I had felt my legs begin to move before I could stop them. I was in the middle of the road when I realized what I was doing, half expecting she might look up and see me even, but my nerves failed me and I scurried back.

She was about forty now. In my eyes she hadn't changed.

Sister Johanna . . . Sister Johanna!

I gave a start. We were almost at the car, which Páll had parked on one of the side streets as usual, but I was away with the fairies.

Do you hear? They're ringing.

Chimes filled the air, and it was obvious from the erratic clanging that something was amiss.

That won't improve his mood, said Páll as he jumped into the car.

ONCE AGAIN I FIND MYSELF FRETTING OVER THE instructions I left for Sister Marie Joseph, worrying that I may have omitted some important details. It even occurs to me that this wasn't so much an oversight on my part as a desire not to give her all the information she would need to properly care for the garden. Although I wouldn't go so far as to say this was a conscious decision, for I'm not as wicked as all that. Instead, I try to recall precisely what I wrote down, because various things I think I might have forgotten to mention keep popping into my head.

I regret once more not having gone down to the stationer's in the village to make photocopies of the list before I left. But I also remind myself that Sister Marie Joseph can't possibly do any lasting damage in the few days I am away, providing she doesn't neglect the garden altogether or make some dreadful mistake. Moreover, I have no reason to think she will, and it is unfair of me to suggest she might. Even so, I am uneasy and wonder whether this might not be because I suspect that my stay in Iceland might turn out to be longer than planned.

The plane is on the runway. I am sitting by the window gazing out into the dark night, as we slowly reverse before moving forward. The delay was longer than expected, and some of the passengers were beginning to show signs of tiredness, complaining to the staff at the gate, even though clearly it wasn't their fault. Fortunately, the seat next to me is unoccupied, and the young girl in the aisle seat smiles kindly at me, before putting on her earphones. I follow her example, and listen to Vivaldi, still wondering whether I might have put less effort into my instructions than I should have.

Furthermore, I cannot help but reflect more on the possible reasons for my oversight. I don't like to brag or call attention to myself in any way, yet I won't deny that over the years I have enjoyed the admiration which the sisters, and others, have shown the rose garden. I have never had to share that admiration with others, and truth be told, I have avoided letting anyone else near it. Whenever one of the novices has shown interest in the garden, I have told them kindly that it is a one-woman job—or words to that effect—or found other ways to discourage them. Since a British journalist visited the area a few years ago and wrote a short article about the rose garden for his publication, tourists have occasionally come here to photograph the roses. We do not object to this; indeed, I make sure to direct them to the chapel afterward, so they can make a contribution to our good causes, if they wish.

And so, over the years, the rose garden has become the convent's pride and joy, and I confess that as a result of this, I enjoy a certain measure of respect. The abbess herself sets the tone, discreetly, of course, though enough so that the others notice.

At first, I tried to deter Sister Marie Joseph from visiting me in the rose garden, but I ended up feeling sorry for her. She was so ingenuous, so eager to help, that I had no choice but to take her on. And she understood my boundaries and her own limitations, she never overstepped the mark, she knew when the lesson was over, and when it was time for her to attend to her other chores.

Perhaps it was a remark Sister Marie Agnès made which put me on the defensive.

I am so glad you have taken Sister Marie Joseph under your wing, she said one morning, when the two of us were alone in the kitchen. I hope she can be of some assistance to you. We are not getting any younger, Sister Johanna.

My arrhythmia is scarcely worth mentioning, and I only occasionally suffer with my arthritis. In many ways I find it easier caring for the rose garden now than when I was younger, for I am more knowledgeable, and moreover it has never looked so splendid. But rather than lighten my load, Sister Marie Joseph has increased my responsibilities, although naturally I am fond of her and want to do all I can for her.

I said as much to the Mother Superior in the kitchen that morning, and we discussed the matter no further. However, something rankled with me, perhaps, sparking a feeling of insecurity that led to me training Sister Marie Joseph less well than I should.

We are preparing for takeoff. The girl in the aisle seat glances at me, and I have the impression that she is a little afraid of flying. I imagine her saying her prayers, hoping that with this servant of God beside her they might count for more. At least that is what I read into her expression, and I try to give her a reassuring smile.

I WAS TELLING PÁLL ABOUT THE ROSE GARDEN, WHEN HE mentioned a former teacher.

He taught at the school for three years, he said. I've no idea why he left. His younger brother and I played football together when we were younger.

Páll wasn't suggesting that this man might have been aware of any goings-on; he simply thought there would be no harm in talking to him.

There must have been other victims over the years, he said. I can't believe this is now happening for the first time.

He looked at me inquiringly, and I nodded back.

I had called the bishop's office that morning to get an answer from him, believing that he had had plenty of time to think things over. His secretary, Hildur, had asked me to hold the line a moment, but then came back to tell me that he was busy and had asked if I could come see him at two o'clock. Páll had arranged to meet the former teacher shortly after and was kind enough to drop me off at Landakot on the way. The snow had been falling all morning; I was fed up with this wintry weather.

Hildur ushered me through to his office the instant I walked in. He was on the telephone.

She's here, he said, rising to his feet, and handing the receiver to me.

I took it, gingerly.

Sister Johanna, a familiar voice said.

The bishop had walked to the door but now suddenly turned around. For a moment I thought he was going to say something, but instead he grasped the handle and disappeared.

Raffin spoke with the same soft voice, and yet his tone suggested that the bishop had troubled him needlessly.

Are you stirring up trouble there in Iceland?

He spoke as one obliged to scold a teenager accused of some minor offense. He could scarcely be bothered, considered it beneath him, even, and yet he had to say something, to sacrifice a few minutes of his precious time.

I asked him whether Bishop Johnson had told him where things stood.

Yes, he says you haven't made much progress.

I see.

Silence.

Do you disagree?

I do.

He waited for me to put across my argument, but I wasn't prepared to give him that pleasure. I knew what he was trying to do, I could sense from his voice that he had already set himself up as the arbiter, the one who would intercede, talk me around, if necessary, play the bishop and me off against each other, make out that he was merely seeking a compromise. But I refused to let him get away with it, this time he would have to stand up and make his position clear.

At last he broke the silence.

He says the boys' parents don't support these accusations, and that they wish the matter to be closed.

That's wrong, I said. The mother of one of the boys admitted that her son told her he had been abused.

Are you sure?

Yes, I'm sure.

That isn't what the bishop told me.

He wasn't there.

Has she made a statement to that effect?

I doubt she is brave enough to do that.

And if she isn't, then what?

I told him I hadn't entirely given up on Karólína Símonar-dóttir, despite the headmaster's threats.

Did she tell you that he had threatened her?

I said she had admitted as much to Páll.

I heard him take a deep breath.

At this point, the bishop is right, he said at last. You have no real evidence.

At that instant, I could have washed my hands of the matter, said farewell to the cold weather, and handed in my report outlining an inquiry that has reached no conclusions. I would have been praised for a job well done in the interests of the church. I could have returned to my rose garden, where work awaited me, and the peace of mind that goes with it. I imagined my cell, the washbasin on the west wall, the view from my window, as the winter sun rises over the hills to the east. The country in hibernation. The mist over the fields. I could have said: Yes, Father Raffin, you are right. We have no real evidence.

And yet I didn't.

I have often regretted it. I regret it now, as I sit on this plane that is making its way across the ocean. For I have no desire to remember those days, which I have spent so long trying to thrust from my mind. I regret it when I lie awake at night listening to the silence, waiting to hear the owl that has made his home in the old barn, in the mornings when I splash water on my face, during the day when I try to concentrate on my roses. And it is no good for me to claim that my refusal to give in was because of those children, for I know that isn't true. I wouldn't let Raffin control me. I wouldn't surrender to him. That was the real reason. That was the only reason.

Do you want me to drop the investigation? I asked.

Sister Johanna, you were assigned a task . . .

You must decide, I said. Do you want me to drop it?

Of course, I knew he would never make that decision himself. Which is why I insisted, and I certainly felt empowered, as I listened to the silence that followed. Until he cleared his throat, and said:

Sister Johanna, you disappoint me. You have been assigned a difficult task, but instead of focusing on that, you prefer to make trips to the countryside . . . And there I was thinking that you had seen the error of your ways and commended your soul to Christ.

I stood motionless after hanging up. The snow was still falling outside.

PÁLL HAD INVITED ME TO HAVE DINNER AT HIS PARENTS' house that evening and told me he would pick me up at Ljósvallagata just before seven. I had accepted gratefully, for I was keen to meet his parents and had also grown tired of my German sisters', and my own, simple cooking. It is true that one of them knew how to make a half-decent meat loaf, but apart from that we ate mostly soup, bread, and cold cuts.

But now I longed to be alone and was thinking of telling him I felt unwell and needed to rest. The other nuns were out, and I stood by my window waiting to see him drive up the street. It was snowing. I felt confused and weak.

Even so, when I saw him park across the street and jump out of the car, something inside me stirred. As if a spark of hope had suddenly awakened in my heart, a belief—not so much in the almighty as in the best things about humanity: optimism, resilience, tolerance—love.

And yet all he had done was park the car, rather badly, leap out with more energy than sense, for he had managed to catch his scarf in the door and had to open it again to free himself. I couldn't help smiling, and as I did so, he looked up and saw me. Instantly, he bent down, made a snowball and threw it at my window.

Needless to say, my plans to stay home alone were scattered to the four winds, and within minutes I was out in the street, and then inside the car sitting next to Páll.

I spoke to the teacher I told you about, he said. He is up to his eyes in work, but we've arranged to meet tomorrow.

Let's talk about something other than Father August Frans, shall we? I said, as we set off toward the suburb of Fossvogur, where his parents lived. He agreed—with what I thought was a sigh of relief—and switched on the radio.

Isn't this the migrant workers' band that was playing when you came to fetch me at the bus station?

He nodded.

Shall I put on something else?

Not at all.

We listened for a while in silence.

They're full of energy, I said.

Too much so, for some people's taste.

They seem to have a lot to say. Not that I understand everything . . .

Probably just as well, he said with a grin.

Do you think they will lose all that fire when they get older?

Isn't that usually the case? People get married, have kids, join the rat race.

I took out my notebook and wrote down the expression "rat race" after he had explained it to me.

What about you, dear Páll? Aren't you going to settle down?

He shrugged.

And this woman friend of yours? The one you went to the cinema with . . .

I don't know, he said. We started going out during our first year at university. Then she went abroad. After that we broke up. We've only just started seeing each other again.

Do you love her?

I could tell he wasn't expecting such a direct question, and I was about to apologize for it, when he replied:

Yes, but that's not always enough.

I refrained from posing any further questions. The migrant workers were singing about the bomb, saying we were all going to die.

They're jolly, I said, and we both laughed.

What about you, Sister Johanna? Did you never fall in love with some boy when you were younger?

Strange though it may sound, his question didn't bother me in the slightest, for I was able to reply with an emphatic no.

You found your faith early on, then.

Fortunately, at that moment, we arrived outside his parents' house, and the conversation ended. I followed him down the pathway to the front door, where they were waiting for us. I knew instantly that I would like it there.

The meal was delicious—roast leg of lamb, potatoes, red cabbage, and pickled cucumber. Páll's parents both had cheerful dispositions, although they were a bit reserved at first, which was understandable. However, I think I broke the ice when I mentioned Jesus, or rather his troubles at Ártúnsbrekka.

I can't believe you told Sister Johanna that you take the Lord's name in vain in that way, his mother said, but then she smiled.

It is a reliable car, I said. And unassuming, I added.

And so the evening went on; we ribbed Páll good-naturedly, spoke of this and that. The subject of my work never came up; indeed, Páll had told them he wasn't allowed to discuss it. I was grateful to them for not being inquisitive, and they studiously avoided any mention of the school or the church.

It felt good to be able to forget everything just for one evening. They opened a bottle of red wine, and although I only drank one glass, I could feel all my tensions and misgivings subside.

It was long past ten when Páll drove me home. My sense of well-being followed me out of the house, and I had a feeling of inner peace, which I hadn't felt for days. I had doubtless long been in need of someone in whom to confide, and, all at once, as I contemplated Páll's profile, his hands gripping the wheel, I felt I had found him. Perhaps it was the glass of wine, I don't know, for I am not impulsive by nature. The words came out by themselves; it was as if I had been waiting all evening for this moment.

I didn't go in, I said.

What?

I sat outside in the car for hours, and when I finally got out, I couldn't pluck up the courage to knock on the door. I stood across the street. It was dark. She didn't know I was coming. I saw her through the window. She was cooking.

I fell silent, and he didn't ask any questions, although I saw him knit his brow. When we reached Ljósvallagata, he escorted me to the door and gave me a brief embrace before we parted.

NEITHER OF US MENTIONED OUR CONVERSATION IN the car when we met after morning prayers the next day. And yet it wasn't as if there was any lingering need for explanations, nor had Páll's behavior toward me changed at all. I had woken up fretting that it might. I feared he would find me pitiful.

He told me he had arranged to meet the former teacher at Mokka and asked whether I would like to accompany him.

Don't you think it might be better if you meet with him alone?

He shook his head, insisting that he didn't know the man that well.

I'd prefer it if you came with me.

It flashed through my mind that he felt sorry for me, and that he was only asking me because of what I had told him the evening before. But those fears dissipated, when he added:

I'm not sure how to broach the subject. I don't want to mess things up.

The teacher, Finnur Logason, had arrived before us and was sitting at a table in the back. He was in his early thirties, tall and thin, with a slight stoop as he rose to greet us. He was surprised to see me but greeted me warmly and was polite though serious. Páll had told me that he now devoted himself to writing and translating and had published two collections of poetry, which had been well received.

When he was in high school, some of his poems appeared in a respected literary journal, Páll had also told me. Us boys were very impressed. I remember these lines, they have stayed with me:

And the day leaves
its shadow
with me.

We ordered our coffees, and Páll and Finnur talked about Finnur's brother and about people they knew in common. I could see that Finnur felt relaxed with Páll, who made him smile a few times.

Then we broached the subject. Páll explained that I had been asked to carry out an appraisal of the school, and that he was helping me. He had thought it might be useful to hear the opinion of someone who knew the school but was no longer associated with it.

So, of course, I thought of you . . .

I only taught there for two years, said Finnur.

Why did you leave? I asked.

I wanted to concentrate on my writing, said Finnur, adding by way of explanation: It was time I did something about it, instead of simply walking around with it gestating inside me.

I said that Páll had spoken highly to me of his poetry. He looked a little uncomfortable, but he certainly seemed to open up after that.

He told us that he hadn't liked the atmosphere at the school. Father August Frans was a stickler for rules and traditions, old-fashioned, and could be quite bad-tempered.

I often found him unnecessarily strict, and he thought I was far too lenient.

What about the other teachers? I asked.

He had most of them in his pocket. Except for Miss Stein. If anything, it was the other way round.

I asked him to explain what he meant.

She's a dreadful old hag. Meddlesome, mean-spirited, and vindictive. She never liked me and gave me a hard time. She and August Frans are thick as thieves. I don't think he dictates to her any more than she does to him.

How are they with the children?

He took a sip of coffee, pausing to reflect, before replying:

Their lives revolve around the school. Nothing else matters. And they run a tight ship.

I had the impression that unless we spoke candidly we wouldn't get much more out of him.

I hadn't ordered anything with my coffee, and all at once I smelled a familiar scent, as the waitress walked by carrying a freshly made waffle with cream and jam. My eyes followed her. They noticed.

Temptation, I said. I must exercise self-control.

They smiled. I reached into my briefcase and took out the letter.

The bishop received an anonymous letter, I said, opening the envelope. I put on my glasses and read out the same accusations I had read to Kristján Hermannsson's mother, Jený.

Finnur's face clouded.

Is it true?

So far we have no proof.

But you think it's true?

He looked at me, then at Páll.

I was about to say that we couldn't be certain of anything at that stage, or words to that effect, but instead I simply nodded.

Yes, I do.

He took a deep breath and raised his cup, but seeing it was empty set it down again.

There was an incident, he said presently, but I am bound by confidentiality. I would need to speak to the person concerned to get his permission to tell you about it.

When do you think you might speak to him? asked Páll.

I'll try straightaway. I'll let you know.

The fact is we've reached an impasse, said Páll. He went on to explain the situation with the boys' families, their parents' response to our probing. Father August Frans is doing everything in his power to stop us, he added.

Finnur listened in silence.

I'll do my best, he repeated, as he rose from his chair and took his leave. But I can't promise anything.

WE'RE EXPECTING A BIT OF TURBULENCE, THE captain announces and requests that the passengers fasten their seat belts. We are about halfway, between Ireland and the Faroe Islands, I imagine. The girl in the aisle seat obeys instantly and grips the arms of her chair. But the turbulence hasn't started yet, and when I look out my window, I see the sun ahead of us and the illuminated clouds which look like scattered ornaments in the sky.

Anxiety is a terrible feeling. I reflect on its ways as I observe the girl out of the corner of my eye, but then I reach into my bag and take out a packet of sweets I bought at the airport. They are lemon-flavored menthol throat pastilles, and after taking one myself, I hold the packet out to the girl. She is deep in thought and gives a start, but then reaches her slender fingers into the bag. She places the pastille in her mouth, and I have the impression that she is no longer holding on quite so tight to the arms of her seat.

I carry on reading the report. Despite having spent the last two decades trying to forget these events, they quickly float up to the surface.

Finnur contacted Páll that evening. He hadn't been successful, but said he wasn't going to give up. He couldn't explain in any detail, spoke again about not wanting to break someone's confidence, and implied he'd had a difficult conversation with the person concerned.

He sounded quite upset, said Páll.

We had no choice but to wait and put our faith in the poet who wrote about the days' shadows. After our meeting at Mokka, Páll lent me the first of two volumes of Finnur's poems, and I decided to spend the evening with them in the living room at Ljósvallagata.

The more I read, the more optimistic I felt, for I thought I glimpsed in his poems a caring, honest soul.

When I met you again
in the January snow
I felt spring had arrived.

Much of his verse was about reflections on love and time, man's place in this transient world, as good poetry so often is. His voice was clear, I thought, and he had something to say. That too gave me hope.

Therefore, I wasn't as surprised as Páll might have expected, when he called me the morning after to tell me that Finnur wanted to meet us together with the unnamed man. He suggested we go to his place, preferably before noon.

I think he is worried the man might change his mind, said Páll.

At ten o'clock we arrived at Finnur's house. He lived in a small, neat apartment in the center of town and received us out in the hallway.

The man was sitting on the sofa, leaning forward, hands clasped. He looked up as we entered and rose to his feet. We introduced ourselves.

He nodded and shook hands with us, rather hesitantly. He was of medium height and strong build and wore blue overalls. His reddish hair was thinning, and the stubble on his face was sprinkled with gray. I was struck by the blueness of his eyes.

He gave the impression that he was eager to get away and had only agreed to meet us as a favor to Finnur. Finnur confirmed this when he said:

I think you should know that Stefán was very much of two minds about whether or not to talk to you. Perhaps it would be more correct to say that he still is, so maybe it's best if you explain the situation.

I realized we didn't have long, and so I got straight to the point. I told him about the accusations in the letter, about Father August Frans's reaction as well as that of the boys' parents. I told him that we had reached an impasse and that we needed his help. He listened quietly, and as I spoke I wondered what he was thinking, but found it difficult to imagine.

When I had finished, he looked at Finnur, then at me.

Did the bishop ask you to come to Iceland because of this letter?

He contacted his superiors, and they sent me here.

Just because of this anonymous letter?

I nodded.

When he looked again at Finnur, I no longer had any doubt about how he felt. His voice was grave, and beneath it was pain and a great deal of anger.

Why did he do nothing when I went to see him? Absolutely nothing.

Eijk has gone, said Finnur. There's a new bishop now.

Stefán looked away. I feared he was about to stand up, when Finnur said:

May I tell them what happened to Magnús?

The man didn't reply immediately, kept gazing toward the window then nodded slowly.

Finnur told us that Father August Frans and Miss Stein had violated Stefán's son, Magnús, when he was a pupil at the school. The abuse continued for over a year, because the boy didn't dare tell anyone about it. However, his parents noticed a change in him. At first they ascribed this to puberty, but finally they decided there must be more to it than that. It wasn't easy to get him to talk, but in the end he told them enough for them to figure out what had been going on.

That was when Stefán contacted me, said Finnur. I had taught his son in fourth grade, and we knew each other from the local pool, where we both went swimming after work. I advised him to speak to Hinriks Eijk, who was bishop at the time.

And did you? I asked Stefán.

Yes, he replied. But he did nothing.

What was his response? I asked.

He told me that children Magnús's age had vivid imaginations. But he promised me he would look into it.

And did he?

I had to put pressure on him. But nothing came of it. He simply repeated that it was a falsehood and advised me to forget about it. He told me this would be best for my son, who needed to concentrate on his studies. Especially math and history, I remember him saying . . .

I was going to ask if he had followed Bishop Eijk's advice,

but stopped myself, because I thought I knew the answer. I also thought I knew that he held himself responsible.

It was as if he had read my thoughts, for he said in a hushed tone: We took him out of the school the following year. But it was just too late.

He made to get up.

I have to go back to work.

It isn't too late, I declared, more abruptly than I had intended. Not if we help one another.

He paused, looking at Finnur as if for guidance. Finnur sat up straight and cleared his throat softly.

What do you propose?

This declaration changes everything, I said.

Stefán's declaration? asked Finnur.

That of his son.

Stefán was clearly taken aback.

What would he have to do? asked Finnur.

He just has to tell the truth . . . In a witness statement.

Before Finnur could reply, Stefán stood up.

No, he said. No.

Without saying good-bye, he strode to the door, followed by Finnur, who obviously wasn't surprised by Stefán's reaction.

They spoke for less than a minute out in the hallway. We couldn't hear what they were saying, but when Finnur came back, it was clear that the news wasn't good.

He told us that for the past few years, Magnús Stefánsson had been having a difficult time. After dropping out of school, he had started mixing with a bad bunch, drinking and using other substances. Moreover, he had been in trouble with the police a few times. He was currently in rehab for the third time in as many years, and his parents wouldn't countenance doing anything that might upset his peace of mind.

If you can call it that, Finnur added. We can assume that these people have done tremendous damage.

We rose from our chairs. There was nothing more to say. Before we left, Finnur felt he had to tell us that when Páll called him he had no idea about what had happened to Magnús after he left the school; he and Stefán hadn't seen each other for years, and he had lost touch with the family.

Had I known, I would never have attempted to arrange this meeting.

Outside in the car, Páll didn't start the engine immediately but gazed out the window, as if he needed to rally his thoughts before he did anything else.

At last he said:

Right now, Finnur is sitting in his living room, blaming himself for not having done more when Stefán went to him all those years ago. Stefán is blaming himself for having failed to protect his son. And we are blaming ourselves for having made no headway. The only person who doesn't blame himself for a damn thing is that wretched, fucking headmaster.

Then he turned the key in the ignition and drove off at speed.

COULD HEAR BELLS CHIMING IN MY SLEEP. I WAS IN THE
rose garden, busy pruning the rambling rose by the old cowshed wall. I pricked up my ears, for there was nothing scheduled in the chapel that day, and besides, the sound wasn't quite
right. On the other hand, I was unable to pay the bells much attention, for despite my efforts, the roses kept growing, until they
were flowing over the wall, and heading toward my old ladies. I
was getting quite concerned and did my best to reason with them,
but to no avail. When I was getting ready to cut them down by the
roots, I finally woke up.

It was five o'clock in the morning, and pitch-black. It took me
a while to get my bearings, but then I realized where the noise
was coming from. I climbed out of bed, opened the window, and
was met by a blast of chilly air and a collision of notes, jangling in
perfect disharmony.

I pulled on some clothes. The German nuns were still in bed,
and I walked quietly to the bathroom and from there into the
hallway, where I put on my coat and the blessed fur-lined boots I
had bought with Páll.

The stars were shining, and it was cold but still outside. The
bells became more muted as I walked up the street, then rang

out loudly again as I approached Landakot. At some point in the night, it had snowed, not much, but enough for me to leave a trail of footprints.

I am not sure what I was thinking when I set off, nor did it become any clearer to me when the church appeared in the distance. Bishop Johnson still hadn't spoken to Father August Frans, and my patience was wearing thin. Naturally, I couldn't have known that I would bump into the headmaster that early in the morning, but I shan't deny that the thought had occurred to me as I stood by the open window in my bedroom, gazing out into the darkness. Nor do I deny thinking that the bishop couldn't reasonably complain if I bumped into Father August Frans by chance and exchanged a few words with him. No, I won't claim that this idea never crossed my mind.

I had just gone past the bishop's office, when the bells went quiet. I instinctively came to a halt, for the ensuing silence was so overwhelming that all of a sudden I felt as if I were alone in the world. I could hear no sound of cars, and the wind was slumbering, like all earthly creatures.

As I approached the church, I noticed that one of the glass windows at the top of the tower had been taken out, and a rope that was hanging from the opening down the outside wall caught my eye as well. Páll had mentioned that parts of the clock mechanism needed replacing, and artisans had been called in to help the headmaster, who was apparently extremely irritated and did nothing but complain.

I was only a few yards away from the church steps when he emerged. I gave a start, but he looked no less surprised to see me, stopping in his tracks, his expression hardening.

Sister Johanna, what are you doing here?

We remained motionless for a moment, then he descended the two steps and stood facing me.

I understood from the bishop that you were leaving. This country isn't for everyone.

I am not leaving, I said. Not before I've done my job.

The lighting along the path cast a faint glow over his face. He wore the same impenetrable smile, his eyes narrower than ever. But his voice had changed. The icy anger didn't escape me.

Why are you here, Sister Johanna? Coming all this way . . .

I was keen to avoid speaking obliquely. He was much better at it than I.

Father August Frans, you know very well why I'm here.

I know that you're leaving and that you have achieved nothing, despite doing your best to sow the seeds of enmity in people's minds. But winter has come, the ground is frozen, and nothing will take root here in this climate . . .

They are children . . .

Children need love and care, he cut in, but what would you know about that, Sister Johanna?

He made as if to leave, and then said:

I've shown you far more tolerance than you deserve. My patience has worn thin. Good-bye.

As I watched him leave, I felt as if everything had gone terribly wrong. Father August Frans had prevailed; he had silenced the boys and their parents, just as he had the church bells, and he would continue on the same path. Nothing could stop him, no one would stand in his way. The bells might rebel again, begin to chime vigorously all of a sudden, but the children and their parents would remain silent.

Before I knew it, I found myself calling after him. It was never my intention, it would never have occurred to me to betray a confidence.

Magnús Stefánsson, I shouted. Do you remember him?

He stopped in his tracks, standing motionless for a moment, without looking back over his shoulder. Stock-still, as though obeying a clear command, but then he continued on his way, if anything quickening his pace.

For my part, I entered the church, where I stood for a while before leaving, not having said a word to God.

THE MIND IS A WAREHOUSE FULL OF THE STRANGEST things, often unbeknownst to me, and so when this or that memory surfaces, occasionally I need to take stock, because for some reason my memories have a habit of contradicting the words on the page, and not necessarily only in the smallest details.

Thus, I vividly recall the German nuns cooking bacon for the very first time when I returned home that morning, after giving away Magnús Stefánsson's name to Father August Frans, and what's more, I can still smell it, if I close my eyes and concentrate. I can also see them before me at the stove, the scrambled eggs on a platter next to the coffeepot, the table laid for breakfast. I clearly remember them inviting me to eat with them, and me refusing, for my excursion to Landakot had taken away my appetite. They were treating themselves, relishing the moment, had doubtless discussed it the evening before, and were looking forward to tucking into their food.

Obviously none of that is in the report, any more than is my exchange with Father August Frans. Nor is it written that this was the last meal the nuns invited me to share with them. Perhaps that is why I can see them so clearly in my mind's eye that morning, while my memory of more important events is sometimes troubled.

We have started the descent. The bright summer night awaits me.

Is it possible that I deliberately distorted some of the facts while writing my report? I believe, hand on heart, that I didn't, although I may very well have gotten some things wrong, for it was as much as I could do to marshal my thoughts at the time. It was Raffin who had asked me to start writing up what had taken place during my stay—that same day, or rather, that afternoon, during a telephone conversation in the bishop's office.

I had tried to imagine what Father August Frans's next move might be. If he feared Magnús Stefánsson coming forward to talk about his experiences, then he would definitely be preparing his defense. On the other hand, I thought it more likely that he would wait and see, assuming I had little evidence, sensing even that I had blurted out his name in desperation.

He heard it in my voice, I told myself, *he knows I was bluffing.*

In the report, it says that I was summoned to the bishop's office the following morning, and yet I am sure that Páll came to pick me up at Ljósvallagata that same day. There is of course no mention of Páll's demeanor; clearly I saw no reason to go into that.

What on earth happened? he asked as I opened the door. I've never seen the bishop so agitated. He wants to see you immediately.

August Frans is defending himself, I said, and relayed to Páll my exchange with him that morning. I hadn't expected this. I thought he would wait and see what happened.

Páll wasn't exaggerating. The bishop was waiting for us in his outer office and dispensed with formalities when we entered.

Didn't we agree that you would wait until I had made my decision?

We followed him into his office.

I told you I needed peace and quiet in order to think, Sister Johanna. Peace and quiet. And now this!

I listened in silence. He went on, becoming more heated.

I assumed Father Raffin had at least talked some sense into you. But no, I see that even he failed. What on earth were you thinking?

Strangely, his words had no effect on me. And rather than flinch when he mentioned Father Raffin, my defiance simply grew stronger.

I asked what he was referring to.

Do you pretend not to know? You lie in wait and pounce on Father August Frans under cover of darkness, when he is wrestling with the church bells. Have you no self-restraint?

Is that all he said?

The bishop looked at me.

Isn't it enough, Sister Johanna?

You are making a big mistake, Bishop Johnson. The man is guilty.

The bishop threw up his hands.

You have no proof. None. My biggest regret is that I didn't throw that terrible letter straight into the wastepaper basket. That was my mistake.

Páll glanced at me. I knew he was waiting for me to tell the bishop about Magnús Stefánsson, and I shook my head discreetly.

The bishop took a deep breath.

Father August Frans has threatened to resign if I don't put an immediate stop to this. I have spoken to Father Raffin, and he agrees with me that the matter should be dropped. You are welcome to speak with him if you require confirmation.

He handed me a piece of paper with Raffin's telephone number on it.

I stood motionless for a moment then decided to call Rome. The bishop motioned to Páll to follow him out of the room.

I have no doubt that he was expecting my call, and yet I had to wait a while before he came to the phone.

Sister Johanna, have you set the cat among the pigeons up there in Iceland?

I wanted to make the conversation as brief as possible.

What do you want me to do?

I cannot oppose the bishop. He sought our help, and this is his jurisdiction. Unless you have proof. Some fresh evidence . . .

I saw no point in mentioning Magnús Stefánsson.

I suggest you spend your last two days in Iceland writing a report on the matter. I expect you to be fair, and don't forget that you have no evidence.

What will happen to him?

I'll do my best. As I did last time.

You mean that he will be transferred to another school, where he can continue his practices?

Sister Johanna. This was your investigation. Neither the bishop nor I stood in your way. You must acknowledge that. You failed. You have only yourself to blame.

Stykkishólmur. He didn't mention it, but the word echoed in my head.

We said our good-byes.

There was no sign of Bishop Johnson when I stepped into the outer office, where Páll and Hildur were waiting for me.

I tried to talk him around, Hildur said, and although I was surprised at the time, it was only afterward that I reflected on her words. She had always seemed so inscrutable, as if nothing would faze her, but just then I noticed a glint in her eye, so fleeting that I couldn't decipher it.

Páll drove me back to Ljósvallagata. The bishop had told him he was no longer required to assist me, and in case there was any doubt about that, he had given him a raft of other tasks.

I shan't take any notice of him, he said, but I tried to smile.

Yes, you will, I said, and, although I didn't quite believe it, I added: Maybe I'll think of something when I put the facts down on paper. Maybe something will come to me.

THE BUS HAS BARELY LEFT THE AIRPORT WHEN THE feeling comes over me that we are on the wrong road. Everything looks so unfamiliar, the lava fields, the wide-open space, the city in the distance. And the glacier, which appears all of a sudden on the far side of the bay, a wisp of cloud floating across it, so thin it is almost transparent at the top. I never saw the glacier last time I was here, I didn't even glimpse it on my way to Stykkishólmur.

Summer night. The light doesn't seem to come from the east or the west, but lies over the land like a blanket, warm but with a feeling that is distinct from sunlight, neither sharp nor hazy, yet almost tangible. You lose your sense of distance, and everything takes on a different hue, even my hands, as I sit on the airport bus. It's as if I'm looking at them through water.

I didn't finish reading the report during the flight but put it aside before I was done. I told myself it made more sense for me to read the closing pages when I reached the guesthouse, alone, with nothing but my memories. Needless to say, the substance is all too familiar; it is the wording I cannot bear to revisit. I have no idea what that says about my inner being.

The guesthouse is on Garðastræti, halfway between Túngata

and Hólavallatorg. It's a house built in the functionalist style, but recently renovated. My room is on the second floor, facing east. I suspect they've only just opened the door to guests, for there is a toolbox in the hallway, the ceiling light has yet to be installed, and when the young man in reception takes me upstairs I can smell paint in the corridor. He confirms this, explaining that they were unable to open in the spring as planned, and that the workmen are finishing off the few remaining jobs.

It is three in the morning and seems if anything lighter out now than on my way in from the airport. My room overlooks a neat garden, and beyond, between two apartment houses, I can see Lake Tjörnin, and up on the hill the Hallgrímskirkja tower. The garden boasts a large expanse of lawn, bordered by birch and rowan trees, low-growing shrubs close to the house, and a few flower beds planted mainly with pansies, if I'm not mistaken. I have never much cared for them myself, although of course they have as much right to exist as all the other plants in God's Creation.

Yet it is the greenery that most catches my attention. Twenty years ago I saw no trace of it.

When I lie down on the bed, I can hear a bird singing in the garden. It's a blackbird, who seems to have a lot to say. He doesn't bother me, though, as I can't see myself falling asleep anytime soon. And yet, I didn't sleep a wink on the plane or on the bus and feel exhausted after the journey. Not to mention the time difference.

No one was waiting to pick me up at the main bus station when I arrived, and I felt rather lost, as if I had been expecting Páll to show up at any moment. Indeed, I found myself automatically looking around for him and the blue Toyota, and even thought

I heard a snatch of the rock music that rang out when he started the car.

Are you a revolutionary?

We wrote to each other a few times then stopped. It was hardly surprising; our last conversation overshadowed all that had gone between us, all the good times. He isn't to blame.

I have been wondering whether I shouldn't get in touch with him. The last I heard, he was married with two little girls, had gone abroad to take his master's degree, and was working for a consulting firm. But that was fourteen years ago.

The new bishop—if indeed I can call him that, for he took over from Bishop Johnson five or six years ago—has asked me to have lunch with him. His name is David Holub, a Czech. I was surprised by his invitation, although my dealings with his office staff have been easy and pleasant, as they seem both friendly and efficient.

I have a book in my suitcase, which I am going to return. The fact that I took it with me when I left shows the state I was in. Light-fingered, I might say, for I didn't ask permission.

I shall take the book with me to lunch and try to make a joke of it when I hand it to Bishop Holub. Somehow it crept into my luggage all those years ago, I shall say, and it is high time it took up its place among the other volumes on the bookshelf at Ljósvallagata—assuming the apartment still belongs to the church. Perhaps I will say something about how lucky I am not to have to pay the daily penalty for late returns—that might break the ice. Or perhaps I should draw as little attention to the book as possible, in case the bishop inquires about my interest in it. Yes, I think it would be sensible to say as little as possible.

The young man in reception asked me if I wanted a wake-up call in the morning, but I told him that wouldn't be necessary. Now I am fretting, because I am still wide-awake, and afraid I will oversleep. Of course, that won't happen, but the thought still plagues me, making it even more difficult for me to fall asleep.

It is light in the room. The curtains barely make a difference. And the blackbird continues his singing in the midnight sun.

FOR A WHOLE DAY, I SAT AT THE DESK IN MY ROOM AT Ljósvallagata trying to order my thoughts on the page with the aid of a typewriter Páll had brought me from the office. Páll was devastated that the bishop had forbidden him to assist me any further. I tried to encourage him, insisting that he should be careful not to lose his job, because I didn't want that on my conscience on top of everything else. He nodded, even attempting to give me a reassuring smile, yet still I felt uneasy.

I found it less difficult to concentrate than I had expected. The typewriter was almost an old clunker, an Erika M, made by a German company in Dresden, as was stamped on it in gilt letters. Fortunately, I had learned to touch-type, but it took me a while to get used to the machine, for the keys were heavy and set rather far apart. Moreover, the "D" was loose and needed to be hit harder than the other keys, although even that didn't always work. This is why that letter is fainter in the report than the other letters, especially early on, for after a while I got the hang of it, and by the end hammering it extra hard had practically become second nature.

By and large, I find my account fairly straightforward, although of course I have been selective here and there, and while in my head I seem to have shuffled some memories around over the years, reading through it now I don't see much I disagree with. I didn't sugarcoat anything and went as far as I could with my assertions, but I chose my words carefully, so that I couldn't be accused of letting my emotions sway my judgment—or run away with me, as Raffin would put it. I was plagued by the thought that he would find some inconsistency and use it to undermine the plausibility of my report, and for that reason it is somewhat drily written, as Páll rightly pointed out when he read it, but at the same time coherent.

By that I mean everything except the end, which I have yet to reread. The two pages I wrote after my return to the convent. I remember it bothering me that the font would be different, separating this addition more obviously from the main text. Of course it didn't matter, but I let it prey on me all the same. Imperial Concorde. That was the name of the typewriter which I borrowed from the Mother Superior.

I was productive that day and scarcely looking up from my desk before I heard the German nuns arrive home in the evening. Even then I didn't leave my room until later, when they were cooking their supper. I was immediately aware of a change in their behavior toward me, and I could only assume that Father August Frans had launched a successful campaign against me. This came as no surprise, and I didn't even bother asking what I was accused of. The report was all that mattered now, and I wasn't about to let anything distract me from that.

They didn't invite me to share their meal, but I had some salami in the fridge and eggs, which I boiled after they had retired to the living room. That was quite enough for me, as I wasn't hungry. Then I sat down again, and carried on into the night, so as not to lose the thread.

When I awoke the next morning, it dawned on me that the noise of the typewriter might have kept them awake, although neither of them had asked me to stop. Páll confirmed this soon afterward, when he stopped by unexpectedly; they had complained to Hildur and asked when they might expect me to move out.

Father August Frans has been slandering you continually since yesterday, said Páll, and is still going strong. He's a cunning devil.

I sensed he was waiting for me to ask what the headmaster was saying about me, but I didn't, for I knew it would fester in my mind, and I couldn't allow that to happen.

I invited him into the living room, and we sat around the coffee table. Clearly something was on his mind, but he seemed unsure about whether to tell me or not.

I'm making progress, I said. They'll be forced to act when they see it in black and white.

He nodded, distractedly. He knew this was merely wishful thinking.

After shifting in his seat for a while, he announced in an impassive voice:

I'm meeting Finnur again later.

Do you think that's wise? I asked.

It was he who got in touch with me.

Why?

He says he spoke to Stefán again. . . .

I gave a start, but he was quick to stifle any hopes:

Stefán hasn't changed his mind, but Finnur thinks he might have something to add.

I was tempted to remind him that we'd been defeated, that there was nothing more we could do, that we ought to stop before any more harm was done. Everything depended on the report now, and I had to concentrate on that; I couldn't allow myself to become distracted by false hopes. But instead I replied:

I read his poems. Many are quite beautiful.

After Páll had left, I fetched Finnur's book of poems, opened it at random, and read a poem that has stayed with me ever since.

There was a misspelling on the headstone
which the moss had not yet
covered.
We spoke of everything
except for what was on our mind.
When we left the graveyard,
hand in hand,
you asked:
Why is it always our mistakes
that linger in our memory?

AWAKE TO THE SOUND OF A DOG BARKING SOMEWHERE in the neighborhood. Half asleep, I imagine George Harrison is calling me, and yet I do not see him anywhere. My surroundings look strange, the field isn't where it should be, and the path that leads home has vanished. When at last I come to, my pulse is racing.

It is half past eight. I've slept for four hours and can feel how weary I am from the journey. The barking soon stops, giving way to the sound of hammering and the din of heavy machinery. Inside the guesthouse it is quiet. I am in no hurry to get out of bed, as I have nothing special to do in the next few hours and I doubt it's a good idea for me to visit my old stomping grounds at this point.

I have tried to avoid thinking about how to spend the next few days. And besides it is pointless, for Unnar Grétarsson will be the one to decide. The bishop's office has been in touch with him, and I am expecting to hear later on when we will meet. I hope it will be today.

"I didn't tell you everything . . ."

He was nine years old, small for his age, blond, with a pale complexion. Like a caged bird, when I found him locked in the broom closet. The teachers had taken the other children over to the gym, and the school was deserted.

I remember that he was shaking all over when I took him in my arms, and that he wouldn't let go when we came out. But that was later—after the ambulance had left and the children's parents had come to fetch them.

But I was shaking, too, and needed the embrace as much as he.

I am restless and unable to stay in bed any longer. When I arrived last night, the young man in reception informed me that breakfast was served in the conservatory until half past nine, and although I'm not hungry, I could at least do with a cup of coffee. Maybe that will perk me up, ease the anxiety that has started to eat away at me.

The sound of the dog barking is still ringing in my ears, and I switch on my phone to see whether Sister Marie Joseph has sent any news of George Harrison. But she hasn't, and I admit that I'm rather relieved.

I take a seat by the window in the conservatory. The guesthouse has eight rooms, and three other guests are having breakfast: an elderly couple and a middle-aged woman. The others have probably set off into town, or to the countryside, for the weather couldn't be better, dry and calm. A young girl comes over to fill my coffee cup and points out to me the buffet, which boasts a selection of bread, cold cuts, yogurt, fruit juice, and porridge. She specifically recommends the porridge, adding that there isn't much left.

I can see now that there is more to the garden than I thought when I arrived last night. Next to the house is a rather large flower bed, which I couldn't see from my bedroom window and which is planted with peonies, dropwort, geraniums, and a variety of buttercup that is very similar to *Ranunculus gramineus*. There might be some room for improvement in the planning, but that is largely a question of taste, for the flowers appear to be flourishing in their present arrangement.

I see that Sister Marie Joseph continued to send messages after I took to the skies last night. I last wrote to her just before eleven o'clock that we would be boarding any moment and I had to switch off my phone. She replied instantly, wished me bon voyage and said something about me letting her know when I had arrived. However, I didn't turn on my phone after we landed—I saw no reason to, as it was the middle of the night in France, and she would undoubtedly be sleeping. *Everything went well, I am having breakfast*, I write, hoping this will satisfy her.

The porridge is lukewarm but tastes fine. In contrast, the coffee is hot, thank goodness, and I gratefully accept a top-up when the girl appears again. She motions toward two small tables in the garden, where she says it's nice to sit when the weather is good. She offers to carry my coffee outside, if I wish. I thank her for her kindness but decide to remain in the conservatory.

I am relieved that Sister Marie Joseph is content to know that I have reached my destination and resists firing off a reply to my message, as is her custom. Perhaps the Mother Superior has scolded her, as she occasionally does when Marie Joseph appears glued to her phone. Or perhaps she is simply busy. At any rate, I am relieved not to have to fuss over the phone for the time being.

It is past ten o'clock when I rise from my chair. I feel rather stiff after my journey, and my arthritis is playing up, especially in my right hip. I had a mild attack of arrhythmia on the way here, but while it is bothersome, there is nothing to fear. Even so, I might stop off at the old cemetery on my way up to Landakot, for I have plenty of time and to be honest I have nothing better to do.

Come what may, I tell myself, as I set off down Garðastræti, leaving the guesthouse behind. And yet these words somehow ring false, for I fear that my anxiety will gradually break down my defenses.

I T WAS AFTER THREE WHEN PÁLL ARRIVED FROM HIS meeting with Finnur. I was still writing and had made quite good progress since he visited me that morning. I had taken a break only to pop out to the grocery story on the corner to buy bread, smoked salmon, and a packet of soup mix, which I had for lunch together with the bread and salmon. It wasn't a bad lunch at all, and when I'd finished eating, I washed up, tidying everything away so as not to give the German nuns more reason to complain.

I had been reviewing what I had written on the antique German typewriter when he arrived. To begin with, I felt quite pleased with myself, for I could find nothing that would detract from the plausibility of the report, or indeed provide Father Raffin with a pretext. However, my relief gradually gave way to a different, less pleasing emotion.

Reading on, it became clear to me that I had failed, that my words merely testified to my own humiliation and impotence. I began to find fault with this and that, insignificant details at first, and then everything of any importance. The writing was flimsy and pusillanimous, the author so painfully circumspect, that finally I had to stop reading. As I thrust the report aside, Páll rang the doorbell.

He looked excited as he walked up the stairs.

He isn't the only one, he declared.

What? I said.

Stefán has told Finnur that his son wasn't the only boy who was abused. He knows of another lad . . .

Do you have his name?

I disliked the tone of my own voice, but it was pointless to try to change it.

Not yet. Stefán hasn't been able to get hold of the boy's parents and won't reveal anything without their permission. I gather he is two or three years older than Magnús.

How likely are they to come forward now if they didn't at the time? I said.

Stefán is doing his best, Finnur says. He feels terrible not being able to talk about his son's experience and wants to make amends for it.

If he feels that bad, he had better get his skates on, because time is running out, I said.

Obviously, I knew how brusque I sounded, and the expression on Páll's face didn't escape me, and yet I refrained from explaining myself or taking back my words. After Páll left, I stood for a long time in the middle of the room with rage simmering inside me. I had become aware of this anger in recent days, but so far I had mostly been able to stifle it, talk myself around, remind myself of what we had actually achieved in the face of much opposition. But this had become increasingly difficult with each day that passed.

It took me a long time to start writing again after Páll had left. Finally, I managed to type a few more words, but rereading them only made me feel even worse.

The nuns arrived home just before seven. I could hear them

out in the kitchen, but I stayed in my room. I had no desire to eat and was unable to concentrate on anything. I simply gazed out the window at the darkness in the cemetery, at the snowflakes falling to the ground in the corona of the streetlamps. At some point I picked up the Bible, but almost immediately put it down again.

I saw when Páll drove up the street and parked opposite the house. The German nuns were watching television in the living room, and rather than invite him into the house, I decided to go and talk to him outside, or even suggest that we drive down to the harbor or around Lake Tjörnin as we had when I first arrived.

I had resolved to apologize for my attitude earlier that day, to confide in him my unease, but I forgot about my intentions the moment I climbed into the car beside him and saw his face. My first thought was that Stefán had gotten nowhere with the other boy's parents, and I was about to give him some words of encouragement, observing that we had more or less expected this, and that he shouldn't upset himself. But he didn't give me the chance, for he spoke first.

Afterward, I couldn't remember in what order the words emerged from his lips, and although, of course, it was of no consequence, this annoyed me. As if I had missed something important. Naturally, I was simply imagining things.

He took his own life. The boy. Three years ago.

It was getting cold inside the car. Páll turned on the engine and switched on the windscreen wipers. We sat for a while in silence, then I said good-bye and went back into the house.

IN PARADISUM DEDUCANT TE ANGELI. . . .

I enter the cemetery at the northeast corner, glancing briefly toward Lake Tjörnin, before pushing open the heavy iron gate. The cemetery is in bloom and leafy boughs stretch in all directions, although many are gnarled with age. The narrow paths benefit from having been laid before the age of urban planners with their measuring sticks; they crisscross the cemetery, some leading to a wall or ending abruptly halfway along, so that more than once I am forced to turn around and search for an alternative route. But at last I find a path leading straight to the little red-and-white bell tower which I remember well from my bedroom window on Ljósvallagata, freshly painted it would seem. I come to a halt, sit down on a bench, and try to open my mind to the stillness, mingled with joyous birdsong.

I am surprised that Sister Marie Joseph hasn't replied to my message by now. Before I left the guesthouse, I asked the young man in reception to show me how to make the phone work when I'm not on the guesthouse's wireless network, in the unlikely event that I needed to use it, and I even jotted down his instructions, just to be on the safe side, although I now discover that this wasn't necessary. I feel almost as if I am sinning when I let temptation get the better of me and press the buttons he showed me. I give a slight gasp when I realize that I've succeeded.

But I needn't have worried about running up unnecessary charges, for I have received no messages from her or anyone else, and no emails.

I have plenty of time before my meeting, and I am not in any hurry. But I'm uneasy and after a few minutes I haven't the patience to sit any longer. I rise from the bench and continue westward along the path.

I have no recollection of the house on Ljósvallagata being yellow. I contemplate it for a while, but then I exit the cemetery on the corner, where I find that the grocery store is still across the street. I don't know what I was expecting, but coming to this area has no effect on me whatsoever, either positive or negative. I suspect that is because it has never left my thoughts, not for very long at any rate. The past is so vivid in my mind that, all of a sudden, I am convinced I see Páll driving Jesus up the street, slowing down as he goes past number 33, as though in search of a parking space. I stop in my tracks, collecting myself only when a blue Volvo rolls by then turns into Hólavallatorg.

I miss Páll. Perhaps that's the explanation, and there is no need to make any more out of this incident. Even so, I am afraid that something will go wrong, that all my preparations will be of little use when I am face-to-face once more with Unnar Grétarsson. He was like a tiny bird in my arms. Perhaps it was I who would not let go of him.

I arrive at the bishop's office just before twelve. His secretary gives me a friendly welcome and ushers me into a meeting room by the entrance. This is a young and soft-spoken woman who asks if I had a good journey, mentions the weather, observing how incredibly lucky I am, because it has been raining almost every day up until recently. I am on the verge of asking her if she knows what became of Hildur, but I think better of it.

I hope she does not sense how I'm feeling, nor indeed Bishop Holub when he arrives a moment later. He is a tall, heavily built man, with a flowing beard and a warm smile. I hope he cannot sense how anxious I am, how I struggle to engage in our initial small talk. On the table, soup and buttered bread awaits us. The bishop has a hearty appetite, while I have none and only manage to eat a little soup and to pick at my bread.

Finally, he brings up the subject of my mission. He tells me he has read my report, but fortunately he doesn't refer to the contents.

A dreadful incident, is all he says, to which I simply nod.

He asks if I remember Unnar Grétarsson. I say that I do, of course, and tell him what he has already seen in the report.

Have you been in touch with him at all since then?

No.

It's strange that he should contact you after all these years.

I nod.

It's too bad that you had to travel all the way to Reykjavík. I offered to meet him myself, but clearly he trusts no one but you. Perhaps it is understandable.

He offers me more soup and serves himself when I refuse. He tells me about his experiences in Iceland, the congregation, how much the school has changed in recent years.

We have a headmistress now, he says. A very diligent woman.

I resist looking at the clock, but he senses that I am getting restless. He clears his throat, pushes his bowl to one side, wipes his mouth, and puts down his napkin.

He lives on the east coast, he says, and can't get out of work till this evening. We only discovered that yesterday, I'm afraid.

I ask when the meeting will take place.

He is driving to Reykjavík after work and will arrive after midnight. So you are set to meet tomorrow morning.

Am I relieved? I don't know. For a split second, possibly, and then my worries take over, the dread of waiting all afternoon, evening, and night.

Unfortunately, he repeats. He had hoped to set off yesterday, but it seems they are short-staffed due to summer vacations.

When I step outside, the sun has burst through the clouds. I set off slowly, but stop halfway across the lawn, raising my hand to shield my eyes. The glare is so intense that suddenly I feel I stand exposed in this blinding light, all eyes upon me, those of God and man, from which I cannot escape.

THE MAN AT THE COUNTER HAD DIFFICULTY CON-
cealing his surprise when I opened the door to the rental
car company, but I have no complaints about his service.
He shows me the various cars that are available and has-
tens to offer me a reduction on a medium-sized Honda, which
he says is practically new and easy to handle. I am used to this
kind of response—a mixture of uncertainty and an exaggerated
desire to please, as if I have a special connection to God, so better
safe than sorry. I don't mean that disparagingly, because the man
seems naturally friendly, and not someone who strikes me as par-
tisan in any way.

My restiveness has brought me here. I had gone back to the
guesthouse and was sitting in my room, enveloped by the deep silence of the afternoon. When the young man in reception handed
me the key, he made the unsolicited observation that the other
guests were out enjoying the good weather—"There's no knowing
how long it will last . . . ," and I had the impression that he was
looking at me as if my behavior were somehow suspect. Of course,
I was simply imagining it, but my restlessness only grew, when I
gazed out my window at the lawn and the gardener, who had just
finished mowing and was now busy weeding the flower beds.

That was when I noticed the book lying on the bedside table, and I realized I had forgotten to return it to Bishop Holub. I had leafed through it that morning while I was still in bed, browsed the photographs of the town, as the dog went on barking. Now I reached for the book again and held it for a moment without opening it. But then finally I made up my mind and decided to go ahead with the trip, which I had been contemplating from the very first moment Cardinal Raffin visited me at the convent and sent me on this journey.

Despite having carefully scrutinized my driver's license, the rental car man gives a look of disbelief as I sit behind the wheel. He reiterates that the Honda is easy to drive and reminds me how good the acceleration is, and that I needn't give it a lot of gas. I thank him for his advice and watch him recede in the rearview mirror, as I drive off.

Sister Marie Joseph helped me to search in the online telephone directory. First she typed the husband's name, and when she couldn't find him in Stykkishólmur, she tried the address. Halla's name alone appeared as residing at 23 Thórsgata.

I tried not to let anything show, as I sat at the computer with Sister Marie Joseph, staring in silence at the monitor.

Is she your friend?

Yes.

Has her husband passed away?

I said I didn't know, that we hadn't been in touch for a long time, and when she found two men with her husband's name, one in the small town of Hella on the south coast, the other in Reykjavík, I pointed out that maybe she had gotten divorced and her husband moved away.

Yes, that is possible, of course, she said, but I could see that the mere idea of this sin made her uneasy.

I told the young man in reception that I was going out of town and wouldn't be back until late that night, or even the next morning.

I gave a start when I blurted this out, for I hadn't even contemplated the possibility myself, not in so many words anyway, but now I couldn't help mentioning it in case someone from the bishop's office tried to get in touch.

It's most unlikely though, I added.

The young man nodded and said he would make a note of it in the computer for whoever was on duty later that day.

And yet, obviously it is entirely possible that she will invite me to stay the night, as I doubt I will make it to Stykkishólmur until well past five. The journey will be shorter than it was all those years ago, because they have dug a tunnel under Hvalfjörður, and the driving conditions couldn't be better, or the weather—the sun is in the sky, the air is calm, and when I drive past Kollafjörður it is as smooth as a mirror. There are quite a few cars on the roads, many with tent trailers attached, and a group of people dressed in exercise clothes crowd the foothills of Mount Esja, preparing to traipse up.

It's remarkable how quickly the sunshine chases my shadows away. I am able to enjoy the here and now and forget what awaits me upon my return; all I can think of is Halla, whom, as always, I see before me encircled by light.

After all these years . . . we will say to each other, and I can feel her presence, as I picture us together.

I am so eager to arrive at my destination that I must be careful not to exceed the speed limit. I did not try to reach her on the telephone before I left, to make sure she would be at home, yet I can feel that this won't be a wasted journey. It actually never even occurred to me to write to her or call, because I need to stand face-to-face with her to know what to say. And perhaps there will be no need for explanations, because time winnows the grain from the chaff, and nothing else matters now but our friendship and the memories we share from the past.

The traffic thins out by the time I reach Borgarnes, because most of the cars are heading north and take a different turn. I allow myself to speed up a little, as the car holds the road well and is indeed easy to handle, as the man at the car rental company rightly said. The landscape looks unfamiliar to me; I saw little of it when I last came this way, and so fortunately it brings back no particular memories. In fact, I could be making this journey for the first time, and that is what I shall have to tell Halla.

The new road over the Snæfellsnes mountain pass is excellent, nothing like the old road in Kerlingarskarð. I almost stop to enjoy the view as Breiðafjörður appears, looking exactly like the photographs in the book. But I am impatient and keep going, barreling down the hill, as I tell myself that I can enjoy the view some other time.

The book lies on the passenger seat next to me. If I am honest, I didn't exactly forget to give it to the bishop, for I remembered it as I had left the room and was on my way downstairs. But then I told myself that since I would be seeing him again, there was no point in going back to fetch it.

The campsites on the outskirts of the town are packed, and there are many cars at the swimming pool. I roll down the windows and hear shrieks of laughter coming from the children queuing for their turn at the water slide. The sun casts its rays onto the streets, and I drive straight to Thórsgata, for I do not wish to risk a sudden change of heart. Not that I really fear that happening, but there is no reason to delay.

I automatically slow down as I turn into her street, but I do not stop until I am outside her house. The garage door is open, and a trailer sits in the driveway filled with all kinds of stuff. The front door is also ajar, and I tell myself Halla must be doing a late spring clean; I have no difficulty imagining her having put it off. I smile to myself, remembering the day she moved into our room; I can see her so clearly standing before me, flanked by her suitcases, not knowing what to do with herself.

I daresay she could do with some help with this clear-out, I say to myself and decide that these will be my opening words when she comes to the door.

I park across the street. I have been driving nonstop since Reykjavík and am a little stiff. However, I soon limber up as I approach the house and am no longer aware of any discomfort as I stand before the half-open door. A rustling noise comes from inside, and seconds later, a woman appears. She looks so like Halla that I give a start.

When she bids me good day, even her voice is familiar.

You must be Halla's daughter, I say. Your mother and I were friends when we were young.

She looks at me, as though trying to figure something out.

Are you Pauline?

That was my name when we knew each other. I took the name Johanna when I became a nun. Your mother and I haven't seen each other for a long time.

She looks straight at me, and suddenly it dawns on me, suddenly it overwhelms me—a split second before she says:

My mother is dead.

HE INVITES ME INTO THE HOUSE. WE SIT IN THE living room. On the floor are cardboard boxes, some full, others empty. She seems more organized than her mother.

The house has been sold, she tells me. I'm handing over the keys next week.

She has taken the paintings off the walls, wrapped most of them in plastic and placed them in the hallway. There is a sheet over the sofa and an armchair in the corner and a piano stands blocking the middle of the room.

The truck driver pulled his back while he and the buyer were moving it, she says by way of explanation. It's being collected to-morrow.

The living room curtains have been taken down, and the sun shines directly onto us.

I'm afraid all I can offer you is a glass of water, she says.

I accept.

Her gestures are familiar, and yet she seems more serious than her mother.

For a moment I thought you were from the local convent. My mother was always very friendly with the nuns.

She has emptied the bookshelves, and yet I see no books.

I sold them all, she says, as one lot, because I have no room for them. Of course, I wish I could have kept them, and the piano—which I learned to play on, but I have a grand now. I teach music.

On my way to the toilet, I look into the dining room. Various knickknacks have been placed on the table, among them some framed photographs. I stop to look at one of Halla in front of the Sacré-Coeur. I took that photograph. She had recently arrived from Iceland.

I feel dizzy, and when I look in the mirror in the bathroom, my face is white as a sheet. I brace myself against the basin and avoid looking at my reflection again. As I stagger back to the living room, I refrain from peering into the dining room.

When my parents divorced, my mother went to Paris for a month, the daughter resumes, once I am seated again. She rented a small apartment, I don't remember where. She told me about you before she left. I think she was planning to look you up while she was there, but she didn't find you. I think she always wanted to live in Paris.

I can't see Halla in this house. I can't feel her presence. Nothing here is reminiscent of her or her spirit. It is as if her mind was never here.

We always assumed she would move to Reykjavík after the divorce, her daughter says, but she never did. Too many things kept her here—her teaching, and of course the family. I am an only child. She was very close to my three children.

From my chair, I can see out to the fjord where a tiny boat is sailing back and forth, as if it doesn't know where it's going. In the distance the islands and islets are turning blue, all but merging with the calm sea.

I found two letters when I was going through her desk, I hear her say, both of them to you. She didn't have the correct address so they were returned undelivered.

She fetches the letters and hands them to me. Printed on both envelopes in delicate script is: *Mme. Pauline Reyer*, while one is addressed to the guesthouse near the Sacré-Coeur, and the other to the flat I moved into after Easter. *Retour à l'envoyeur* is stamped on both.

My mother must have opened them, because I didn't. Oddly enough, I don't speak any French. I studied German at school. An act of rebellion, maybe . . . And because of music of course. Bach and Brahms and Schubert and Beethoven. Mozart . . . I felt I need to understand their language. But the main reason was probably rebelliousness.

Like her mother, she thinks out loud, says whatever comes into her head. And yet she seems less dreamy than Halla.

Why would Halla have opened the envelopes? To check on something or did she simply want to relive the past perusing her own words. Perhaps in the tedium of a quiet afternoon, where nothing awaits but evening, the sleep that follows, and the realization that all the next day will be exactly the same as the last. Then did she open the letters, as she might study faded photographs hoping to conjure up forgotten moments, something that no longer mattered, but could help her while away the time on a quiet day?

I finger the envelopes, then place them in my bag.

Finally, they have been delivered, the daughter says, as she follows me to the door. My mother would have liked that.

She puts her arms around me when we part. The embrace lasts longer than I might have expected, and I return it warmly, for somehow I feel as if I am also saying good-bye to her mother.

I think you were always in her thoughts, she says. I have the impression that she is about to say something else, and I am almost relieved when she doesn't.

THE BLACKBIRD SINGS IN THE MIDNIGHT SUN.

There has to be an explanation hidden somewhere, albeit confusing and ambiguous, for the thought that my entire life has been built upon a misunderstanding is too cruel. Surely the meaning will one day become clear, placing my life in the appropriate context, where everything will be impartially judged, my mistakes doubtless examined, but some mitigating circumstances taken into account as well.

In the end, the tide of forgetfulness washes over us all. The words we spoke no longer echo in anyone's head, the things we left unsaid no longer matter.

The letters lie on the table in my room, the ink faded. They are alike, in some passages identical. The second one is longer.

"Dear Pauline . . . it has been four months since we parted, and I thought that time would have put everything in perspective by now. But nothing has changed—I feel exactly the same . . ."

After she had left, I started to sketch portraits of her. I don't know where the idea came from, as I have never been any good at drawing. I didn't use a photograph because I wanted them to be from memory, or perhaps to be sure that I hadn't forgotten anything, not a single feature. I seem to recall that the result wasn't bad, yet I was never satisfied and persisted until I felt it had become an obsession. In the end I had to force myself to stop. I don't think I have sketched anything since.

". . . Maybe I shouldn't be telling you about my feelings, maybe you don't want to know. But I can't help myself; all my efforts to repress my thoughts have failed. Forgive me . . ."

I didn't open my bag to take out the letters until I left Stykkishólmur. Just outside the town, a small stream runs beneath the road, winding its way down to the sea. Farther on is a pull-off, where I parked the car facing east, so I wouldn't have the sun in my eyes.

I hadn't expected to discover anything new in these letters, nothing she hadn't already written to me just after she arrived back in Iceland that summer, or in the letter she sent when she started at the university. Even so, I felt anxious as I put my glasses on and opened the first letter, dated October 3.

Forty years are wiped away. I have moved into the tiny convent in the nineteenth arrondissement, and the Mother Superior has given me permission to change cells, because the cell I was first allotted has a bad mildew smell. Outside the air is crisp, but it is sunny. I am still getting used to the neighborhood, the new faces and routines. The Mother Superior is strict. I'm having a hard time controlling my thoughts and look to my communion with God for consolation. I beg him to help me take hold of myself, I beg him to change me so that I stop thinking about Halla every moment of the day.

But she is still writing to me.

The course of my life . . . Years turn to days, and days to moments. I look back over the path I have traveled and see that it is no more than a minute thread vanishing into the blueness. And the end point? That is here, in this pull-off outside a small town, where I discover that my entire life has been built upon a misunderstanding.

Despite all my confessions, the questions remain the same and the answers as unsatisfactory as ever. From now on nothing will change, nothing will be taken back, nothing added.

"I thought these feelings would fade . . ."

I do not pity myself, nor do I wish to be pitied by others. Sympathy can be like a resounding slap, and when at last I drive up to the guesthouse and park the rental car outside, my biggest fear is that the young man in reception will see the meaninglessness of my life in my expression. That is why when he hands me the key to my room I smile and make some comment about the weather as I say good night.

The blackbird is singing. I lie awake. Just before morning it starts to rain.

I WAS WALKING AWAY FROM THE CHURCH WHEN I SAW him at the window. I didn't come to a halt immediately but turned around after several steps. I couldn't help myself.

The ambulance had left, but the police were still on the scene. They hadn't started to clean the blood off the ground. That was later.

The teachers had taken the children into the gym, all except Miss Stein, who had broken down and been carted off.

I don't know how I caught sight of him. Only his hands and the upper half of his face were visible. He was completely still; I couldn't read anything from his eyes.

I walked into the deserted school building. A deep silence hung over it. I stood in the hallway listening for him but couldn't hear a thing.

I tried one door after another, until I came to the broom closet. The key was in the lock, and I turned it gingerly before opening the door.

He didn't look around but continued to stare out the window. He was standing on tiptoe on an upturned bucket, clutching the windowsill. I walked over to him slowly then placed my hand gently on his shoulder.

He shuddered, and I felt his body go rigid. Slowly I prised his fingers away from the windowsill and lifted him off the bucket. He offered no resistance, and I sat cradling him on the floor.

Gradually, he relaxed, until he lay limply in my arms. I held him tight, caressing his brow and his cheek as softly as I could. There, there, I repeated, for I could think of nothing better to say. There, there.

I don't know how long we sat there, as I lost all sense of time. Only when we were discovered by a police officer on his way to the headmaster's office did we get up.

Or rather I did, for Unnar was unable to stand. I carried him out to the hallway, where I waited while the police officer went to the gym to fetch his teacher. They hurried back, and the teacher, a middle-aged woman, apologized, claiming she thought the boy was in the care of Miss Stein.

He refused to go to the woman and held his arms tightly around my neck. He hadn't said a word, and that was not about to change. The teacher popped out, saying she was going to call Unnar's grandmother.

He lives with her now, she explained.

I sat down with him on a chair by the entrance. Soon his grandmother arrived. She was about sixty, a woman of few words, unassuming; the boy let go of me at last when she held her hand out to him.

I watched them leave the school and walk down Túngata, where they turned the corner and I lost sight of them. He had wet himself, and I hoped they wouldn't meet any of his classmates on the way. He seemed so terribly small.

Later that day I was summoned to the bishop's office. Unnar's grandmother had been in touch with his teacher and told her the boy appeared to have seen what happened from the window in the broom closet. He had blurted it out when he finally recovered his speech. The teacher, who was aware that no one else had witnessed the incident that morning, had informed Bishop Johnson. And now the police and the bishop were waiting for the boy and his grandmother in the bishop's office. Unnar had asked if I could be present.

All these years later, I am now making my way to the same place to meet him. At ten o'clock. A grown-up man. In the meeting room next to the entrance, I assume. I haven't slept, I feel numb as I chase my own feet up Hávallagata.

The rain hasn't let up. As I was leaving the guesthouse, the young man in reception offered to lend me an umbrella. I declined. I haven't far to go, I explained, but then I stood in the doorway for ages, contemplating the rain. Only when he repeated the offer, clearly believing that I was waiting for it to stop, did I set off.

The cathedral clock strikes ten. I count the chimes and at the very last moment decide to make a detour on my way to the bishop's office.

AT LAST I FELT YOUR PRESENCE. NOT IN THE GLIMMER of light that was barely capable of illuminating the colors in the stained-glass windows or in the sufferings of your son on the cross above me, not even in the words of the psalms that refused to quicken in my mind.

I enter your house empty-handed. My palms are cold.

Come and see God's works, the psalm says. I have seen them, and I do not like them. On life's journey, men are not who they were when they set off, or who they will have become when that journey ends. You taught me to feel ashamed of myself, you taught me to look away, to avoid people's gaze. No crime is too wicked to be concealed, as long as it has been carried out in your name. And there will be life after death if we do your bidding.

I wish I could say that I no longer believed in you, but your image is now clearer than ever before.

Your justice is more merciless than man's injustice. You speak of love and show us the sun to give us hope. But then autumn arrives, the grass withers and the flowers fall, and after that it's winter . . .

I heard the German nuns get up. It was five o'clock. It must be said that they moved about quietly, hardly making a noise, and by six o'clock they had left for church. I waited, having not slept a wink, the finished report on my desk. I had left nothing out, not even the suicide Páll had told me about the night before, although I knew it would change nothing. Perhaps he would be transferred. Perhaps not. I couldn't be sure about anything, and Raffin was pulling all the strings.

Your justice . . .

I was eager to speak with you, but I waited until it was almost eight o'clock. By then the German nuns and everybody else who had attended early morning prayers would have left the church. I knelt and crossed myself and tried to feel your presence, I waited for the light to set ablaze the colors in the windows. But it was only when I stopped looking and accepted that no light would be streaming in that I felt you. In the gray of the morning. With the prayer book in my hands, unopened.

My rage set me free. In it I found consolation. In my defiance against your righteousness.

Suddenly, while we were conversing—or rather while I was conversing with you, for you never answered me—the bells started to chime. I was startled, and when I looked up, I saw the church door open, and Father August Frans hurrying toward the stairs up to the tower.

Was this a coincidence, or had you blessed me with your providence? Had you brought him here, so that I could look him in the eye before I surrendered, packed my suitcase, left the country? Was this your reward, a brief exchange with the priest, if only to appease myself?

I rose from my pew and followed him. The door was ajar, and I started up the narrow spiral staircase after closing it behind me. I didn't see him, but paused to catch my breath when I reached the loft, where the organ and the choir balcony were. From there, a steep flight of steps led up to some stained-glass windows on the right which faced west and were if anything paler than those surrounding the altar. I had to stop while my eyes became accustomed to the darkness, and when at last I reached a short, narrow passageway, it took me a long time to find the corner door that led me up another staircase, this one made of stone.

I have always had a fear of heights, but so determined was I to reach the top that I thrust aside my fears, not once looking back.

The bells were still clanging, disharmoniously as before, but without the same urgency. They would start all of a sudden and then stop just as abruptly, with lengthy pauses in between. But the noise became more and more unbearable the higher I climbed, and each time the clapper struck home, I had to clasp my hands over my ears, even though I needed them to crawl up the wooden staircase that came next and was even more perilous than the one behind me.

Stopping at the top, I saw a double trapdoor, one flap of which was open. In the light seeping from above, I glimpsed the bell chamber, and when I sharpened my ears, I could hear footsteps. I gathered up my skirts to avoid stepping on them and made my way slowly up the remaining steps.

He was struggling with the bells, had gotten hold of one of the clappers, and was winding a piece of sacking around it. Behind him I saw a hole in the wall, where the window had been removed and propped up against the wall. The ropes I had seen dangling outside were fastened to a steel girder that held up the bells. It was cold up there, and every now and then the wind would blow snow into the chamber.

He hadn't seen me, and I stood for a while in the shadows watching him. I had been in such a hurry to get up there, but now my tongue was stuck to the roof of my mouth and refused to move when I tried to clear my throat. Not because I was frightened of him, but rather because my anger had rendered me speechless.

There he was struggling with the clapper, but what was he thinking, what secret plans was he concocting, which fresh victim did he have on his mind? There he stood, sacred and untouchable, having demonstrated his superiority and my weakness. Calm, without a care in the world.

The wind was whining in the bell chamber, and when Father August Frans had finished wrapping the clanger in sackcloth, he stretched, turning toward the opening in the wall. Perhaps he was contemplating his next task, for he took hold of one of the ropes and adjusted its position, or perhaps he was admiring his domain.

All these things will I give to you . . .

He didn't notice me until I had circled the bells and was almost upon him. Even then he didn't give a start, but smirked instead, as if he had been expecting me and relished reminding me of my humiliation, smirked to my face, standing his ground until I stepped forward.

It seemed to take forever for him to lose his footing. He tried to grab me, but I stepped aside, the wind blowing my skirts in the open window as he toppled. Suddenly, I felt I might fall with him and I had to brace my legs and grab the casing to steady myself.

I stood there shivering, as I watched him disappear through the falling snow before he crashed to the ground. And there he lay without moving, a black speck on the white snow.

THE WIND HOWLED INSIDE THE COLD BELL CHAMBER, but otherwise there was a deathly hush. To begin with I couldn't move but kept on staring at the speck on the lawn, the school on the other side of it, the city stretching toward the sea, looking gray in the falling snow. There was no movement around the school or the church.

When my muscles finally relaxed, I stepped backward, very slowly, for the slightest movement felt exhausting. I rested for a moment next to the bells, but when my mind began to clear, my first impulse was to flee. Where I didn't know.

The thud echoed in my head as I clambered down the tower, resounding louder the farther I descended. I stumbled once, at the bottom of the wooden steps, but I only fell a short distance. Still, I scraped my palms, but only noticed they were bleeding once I was back inside the church.

It was empty. I had left my prayer book on the pew, and I sat down there once more and waited. It seemed like a long time before I heard the wail of sirens out in the street. An ambulance or a police car, I assumed, possibly several judging from the din. But then they fell silent, and no sound entered the church, nothing to drown out the pitiless words that had started to echo inside my head.

At last you spoke up. At last you let me feel your presence.

I entered your house empty-handed, but I leave bearing your gifts . . .

After about half an hour, I heard the church doors open. Two men walked in, the deacon and a police officer, who headed straight up to the bell tower. They came back down after a little while, the deacon locked the door after them, and then they left.

Shortly afterward, I rose to my feet and went over to the door. I could only see outside if I opened it, and I waited for a while before summoning the courage. There was nothing to see except a police car that had parked up on the sidewalk on Túngata. The ambulance was most likely long gone, and any onlookers that might have gathered around had also disappeared.

I clutched my prayer book, as if it proved beyond doubt my reason for being in the church. There was blood on it, and I could feel it sticking to my palm. I walked out onto Túngata, past the police car, and along the path crossing the lawn. I kept looking straight ahead until I had passed the school, and then, out of the corner of my eye, I saw a movement in the window of the broom cupboard.

Later on, I wondered why I hadn't simply walked down Túngata, and then doubled back around the church toward Ljósvallagata. Some might say God's guidance; I say habit. I simply lacked the strength to change direction. It was as much as I could do to keep from collapsing.

When I first took him in my arms and slid to the floor with him, I couldn't work out if it was he or I who was shivering and trembling so much. But then I gradually realized and managed with some effort to take hold of myself.

I was packing my suitcase when the telephone rang, and Hildur summoned me to a meeting with the bishop. The boy had found his voice, she said, but he refused to speak to anyone unless I was there. Could I come to the bishop's office at three o'clock?

I sat on the bed in my room. My flight left the following morning, and my ticket lay on the desk together with my passport and the report, which I hadn't yet handed in. I picked up my ticket and stared at it for a moment before putting it down again. Outside, it was still snowing.

Father August Frans hadn't made a sound when I pushed him, he hadn't screamed, he hadn't shown any sign of weakness or fear. He had only tried to take me with him when he fell.

Unnar and his grandmother were already sitting in the meeting room when I arrived. Bishop Johnson, however, was waiting for me out in the corridor, together with a middle-aged police detective, who had a rather abrupt manner. I thought I saw the bishop give me a reproachful look, and for a split second I was terrified he might have guessed the truth. But then I collected myself: of course, he would associate the headmaster's suicide with my assignment in Iceland. Even so, I didn't breathe any easier.

The boy looked so tiny sitting at the big table. I greeted his grandmother, then patted him on the head, and sat down beside him. Bishop Johnson and the detective sat opposite us. They tried to smile, but of course the boy was terrified. I was going to suggest that we might be more comfortable sitting on the sofa in the bishop's office, but I didn't.

The detective started gently. He asked the boy his age, whether he enjoyed school, how he liked the snow, and other similar questions. Unnar sat with his hands in his lap, head bowed, replying in words of one syllable wherever possible. His grandmother watched him while he spoke, avoiding looking across the table.

When the conversation turned to his spell in the broom cupboard, he clammed up, because the detective made the extraordinary blunder of asking what he had done to merit being shut in there. He soon realized his mistake and tried to correct himself, adding that he had often been made to sit on the naughty step when he was a boy. But Unnar was on guard now, and only after a pause, during which unrelated things were discussed, was the detective able to turn the conversation back to the events that morning.

It was then that Unnar fumbled for my hand beneath the table. I clasped it gently in mine, caressing the back of it with my thumb.

Suddenly, he raised his head and looked me straight in the eye. It was as if he were seeking guidance—my permission to speak of what he had witnessed. I grew nervous, though I did my best not to let it show, and gave him a nod of encouragement, I suppose, for I knew they were all looking at me and I had no choice.

Batman, he said.

What? said the detective.

I thought it was Batman.

The detective frowned, and then the boy's grandmother stammered, as if each word might get herself and the boy into trouble:

He reads comic books.

Comic books? the detective repeated.

Yes, she said.

And you thought this was Batman . . . ?

I know it wasn't him, Unnar blurted, as if he were taking an oral exam and wanted to show the teacher that he knew the subject. I know it was Father August Frans.

Father August Frans usually wore a black suit, with a gray jumper underneath, so that you could just see the top of his collar. I waited for the detective to ask Unnar why he had thought it was Batman, what it was about the headmaster's appearance that had given him that impression.

But instead, he said:

Did you see him up in the tower for long?

A little.

And what was he doing up there?

I don't know.

The bishop had taken a back seat, but now he glanced toward me. I could feel his eyes on me, and although I didn't return his gaze, there was no mistaking what he was thinking. I was the culprit. I was responsible for this mess.

Was there anyone with him?

The boy must have felt the shudder that went through me, but he gave nothing away and shook his head resolutely—too quickly, I thought, as if he wanted to make sure he wouldn't be asked any more questions in that vein.

At least that was how I saw it, although later on I wondered whether he had noticed me at all at the open window. It had been snowing, and I told myself his eyes must have followed the headmaster all the way down and stayed on him when he crashed to the ground.

The detective had no reason to dispute the boy's testimony. He moved on as though afraid the boy might clam up again.

Then what happened?

This time, the boy didn't respond straightaway, but knitted his brow as if he were trying to remember something important or find the right words to describe it.

He just flew down, he said at last.

I instinctively squeezed his fingers and then stroked the back of his hand as gently as I could.

Bishop Johnson straightened up in his chair, as though making to get up, for there appeared to be nothing more to say.

And then Sister Johanna found you in the broom cupboard, he said, as if for good measure.

The boy nodded.

The detective looked at the rest of us, and when he seemed satisfied that he had covered everything, he thanked the boy and his grandmother for coming, adding a few words of encouragement, which I suspect were lost on them.

I took my leave of them outside, and when Unnar's grandmother was about to lead the boy over the lawn, past the school and the church, I suggested she perhaps take a different route. She understood, and I watched them walk hand in hand in the other direction, down Hávallagata. I was half expecting the boy to look back, but he didn't, and after they turned the corner, I stood for a long time before I finally got going myself.

PÁLL. I HAVEN'T FORGOTTEN TO MENTION HIM, BUT rather I have put it off. I often think of him while I am tending my roses, or as I lie in bed in the evenings waiting for sleep to come. Sometimes, I wake up with him in my thoughts, and then it's as if he's there, but the tangle of dreams soon unravels and I am forced to face the truth that I left him in a lurch.

I betrayed him. That is what I did. I took advantage of his trust, and his affection for me—I sacrificed him.

Knowingly? I ask myself as dawn breaks and the first rays of sun light up the sky above the hills to the east. In the evenings when darkness encircles me. *Knowingly?*

I had arrived back at Ljósvallagata. Fortunately, the German nuns were out and the stillness of afternoon filled the apartment. After saying good-bye to Unnar and his grandmother, I had fetched the typewriter, and returned it to Hildur.

The bishop was nowhere in sight, and I decided not to ask her about him. I reminded her that my flight left the next day and told her that I saw no reason to postpone it, asked if anyone had suggested I do so.

She shook her head, and suddenly I noticed the change in her

demeanor; she wasn't just upset, which would have been understandable, but seemed on pins and needles. She took the typewriter from me and put it away. I sensed something was on her
mind, and yet she said nothing, until I had reached the entrance
and was about to grasp the door handle.

Sister Johanna, she said all of a sudden, Sister Johanna . . .

I turned around, at which she hesitated, wishing perhaps that
she had kept silent. But then she found her voice, filled now with
remorse and dread.

Could this all have been a misunderstanding?

I knew instantly to what she was referring, and at last I understood her part in this, at last it dawned on me: "Hildur knows
everyone and everything," Páll had said.

I looked at her for a moment, even as I tried to gather my
thoughts, then I gave her the resounding reply she had earned.

No, I said. This was no misunderstanding.

I don't know whether my words made her feel any better, I
couldn't tell. She said nothing, but watched as once more I made
to open the door, the expression on her face unchanged. I paused,
and before I realized it, uttered the words that had been echoing
in my head all day.

I regret nothing.

Was I talking to her or to myself—or to you, who watch over
us without mercy, waiting for us to sin? Was I comforting myself
or declaring war on you? Who knows?

And nor should you, I said, and walked out.

There was nothing for me to do at Ljósvallagata. I had packed
my suitcase—a simple task—and now I was counting the hours
until my flight. The evening and the night ahead, the ticking
clock; and then my departure.

I was surprised by Páll's absence, and yet I hadn't asked about him when I was summoned by Bishop Johnson, along with Unnar and his grandmother, or when I took the typewriter back. I had felt relieved not to have to look him in the eye, because I didn't know if I would be able to conceal the truth from him.

And so, I gave a start when, standing by the window, I saw him drive up the street and park outside. He stayed in the car, although it didn't look as if he was doing anything, just sitting still, staring straight ahead.

At last he got out and walked up to the house. I hesitated before letting him in, and it actually occurred to me not to answer the door. But of course I did, and by the time he came up the stairs, I had composed my expression.

We sat in the living room.

I didn't see you today, I said.

I came into the office late, he said in a hushed voice.

He looked downcast, as was to be expected, and avoided my gaze. I wasn't surprised that he was troubled by remorse; I knew the feeling only too well. And yet his manner struck me as odd; I was bewildered by the distance that had suddenly arisen between us.

I longed to take his hand, to give some words of reassurance, to embrace him. And yet something prevented me.

I'm leaving tomorrow as planned, I said instead. There is no reason for me to stay on.

He didn't reply, he didn't even nod, just kept staring straight ahead. I could sense that something was churning around in his mind, something he couldn't express, although he kept trying, and the effort was visible on his face and in his gestures. He looked as if he was being crushed by a great weight. *He thinks we are responsible for the way things turned out*, I said to myself. *He feels guilty.*

Seeing him like that made me feel bad, and I was going to say something to break the silence when all of a sudden he looked up.

I saw you, he said.

I gave a start.

I saw you leaving the church.

That was all. Just those few words. We sat in silence, he said nothing more, and I felt too weak to respond. At least that is what I've told myself whenever I've been assailed by doubt, tormented by guilt, too weak to confess to my crime, too attached to my own skin.

I still don't know what he was after. Perhaps he didn't either. He had no more words, and when I saw him to the door, I felt that I had lost his friendship forever.

I'll take a taxi tomorrow morning, I said. It's an early flight.

He paused in the doorway then gave me a fleeting embrace. I wanted to hold him tight, but he freed himself before I had the chance.

AS IN A MIRROR. IN A BLURRED IMAGE. AFTER ALL these years . . .

I have prayed to you with all my might, I have suffered remorse; I have decided that the world would be a better place without me. I have sought but not found, and forgiveness is always beyond my reach. When I lean over the washbowl, I only see the outlines of my face.

The gray morning light seeps into my cell, as the moon fades in the sky. Somewhere, a soul has woken in need of comfort. Somewhere, I would have led a different life.

My face remains still in the cold water.

I believe in man's goodness, and evil. I don't believe in absolution, eternal life, your mercy. I have seen a hand caress a cheek, and a fist ready to strike. And you always keep your distance.

I still feel the physical contact. It comes without warning, and I snatch my hand away, as if a thorn has pricked me. But I'm always too late, both awake and asleep. The black speck on the ground.

Do I believe in you? I do not know. And yet I continue to speak to you, despite knowing that you offer me no atonement. I no longer seek it, and do not fear my lack of remorse. Sleep comes and goes.

As I had expected, Raffin shelved my report.

We must each interpret his suicide in our own way, he said. I understand that conscience compelled you to make the case against him in your report. But since Father August Frans is no longer here to defend himself, the matter is closed.

He insinuated that I had manipulated the report to absolve myself. Indirectly, of course. I was tempted to remark that I had already finished my report before Father August Frans died, but I realized it was pointless and said nothing.

I suggest that you write up your account of the accident in an addendum, he went on.

I took a taxi to the bus station. It was cold that morning, and I hadn't slept all night. I remember little of the journey to Keflavík airport.

I wrote to Páll about a month later. I told him a little about daily life at the convent, spoke about the weather. The letter had a bland tone. I only mentioned my stay in Iceland at the very end, when I urged him not to let our friendship influence him, to follow his conscience. Word for word and to the point, no beating about the bush.

"I think of you often. I see you before me, driving up the road in Jesus, and I remember all the good times we had. But you mustn't let our friendship influence you."

Thus, I told myself, I had done my duty by him, and for a while I believed it. But then, of course, I realized that it was the exact opposite. And so? So I did nothing to rectify matters.

His reply was brief and courteous. He told me he had left his job at the bishop's office and was working in construction. In the fall, he would begin his postgraduate studies. He said nothing about what had happened to us during our time together, but mentioned that he had taken Jesus to the mechanic the day before he quit.

Time frequently stands still, even though the years fly by, and before we know it things have come to an end. Sometimes, I feel I have traveled a long road only to end up where I started. But there are brighter days, when George Harrison and I are untroubled by shadows, and my roses remind me of the magnificence of Creation. Those days come, and then night plunges me into a deep and dreamless sleep.

MAKE A DETOUR. THE CLOCK STRIKES TEN, BUT I'M reluctant to quicken my step. I regret not having accepted the offer of an umbrella from the young man in reception, because the drizzle is relentless, and it doesn't look as if it will let up anytime soon.

I'm not ready for the bishop's office, so I walk down Hóla-vallagata, and from there up Túngata toward the school and the church. It's summer break so the school is deserted—no lights in the windows, no children coming or going. Sadly silent.

On the path between the school and the church, I pause on the exact spot where I noticed Unnar twenty years ago. I contemplate the broom cupboard window a few yards away, then turn slowly and let my eyes slide up the tower—as so often in my thoughts these past weeks.

However, it looks alien to me in the gloom, darker than in my memory, taller and closer. When I was a child, a tussock of grass appeared as a mountain, and perhaps that is happening to me again. It looms over me, and all of a sudden I feel the urge to retreat, although of course there is nowhere for me to go.

Did he see me? After all these years, after all my deliberations with you, dear God, and with myself, the sleepless nights, the doubt, the search for remorse and forgiveness, after everything that has come to pass, this is the question that has thrust all others aside.

Did he see me? Is he ready to identify me?

The ropes are long gone, the stained-glass window has been reinstated, dark in the drizzle, as are the walls. I cup my hand over my brow and sharpen my eyes, but I am no closer to the truth.

How should I know what a child's eyes saw? Why speculate when the answer awaits me in the bishop's office? Why?

Even so, I pause, take one step forward and another back, rub my eyes, stare up at the window where twenty years ago I struggled with the icy wind.

At last, I continue on my way. I am ten minutes late, but I do not hurry, needing the time to collect myself before I go in.

I take off my damp coat in the hallway and wipe the rain from my face. The bishop's secretary comes to greet me, as cheerful as before, and doesn't allude to my being late. Nevertheless, I apologize, explaining that I had to run an errand on the way and underestimated the time it would take. Those are my exact words, and she doesn't query it, but lowers her voice slightly.

Unnar arrived here early, she says, and is waiting for you in the conference room. The bishop is there too.

The door to the meeting room is open, and as I approach, I can hear their voices. I slow my pace, and so does the secretary, giving me what seems like a reassuring smile. She is just being polite, of course.

He looks up the instant I appear in the doorway. Bishop Holub turns toward me.

Sister Johanna, he says cheerily.

Unnar stands up. I am speechless, and I stare at him as he approaches me holding out his hand. He is of medium height, slim, with a well-manicured beard and a receding hairline. Thirty, but looks older. He doesn't remind me of the little boy I held in my arms in the broom cupboard, until I look into his eyes.

I shake his hand, forget to let go, and he seems in no hurry to withdraw it.

You've grown a little, I manage to say.

He smiles.

You are exactly the same as I remember you, Sister. Exactly the same.

His words startle me, for no reason, I hope, but I try to hide it.

We sit down.

We were talking about the fjords on the east coast, says the bishop. Unnar has been living there for over ten years.

Yes, twelve, he says.

I was just asking Unnar about the famous fog. Have you heard about it, Sister Johanna?

I tell him I don't think so.

Yes, the famous East Fjord fog, the bishop repeats. According to what I've read, it's a rather remarkable phenomenon.

It comes and goes, says Unnar.

Silence.

Forgive my lateness, it occurs to me to say at last. I was detained.

It's good of you to come all the way from France to see me, says Unnar. It has taken me a very long time to pluck up the courage.

He doesn't appear timid, and yet his delivery feels rehearsed, which makes sense when he adds: My therapist has helped me a lot. He encouraged me to go through with this.

It isn't clear what he means. Encouraged him to go through

with what? This meeting with me? Telling the truth? Dealing with his past, I believe is the expression?

"I didn't tell you everything . . ." he had written in his letter.

The bishop's secretary enters the room bringing coffee and some biscuits on a plate.

Ah, a little snack, says the bishop, perking up. Thank you, Dísa.

He serves the coffee, while we watch in silence.

Perhaps you two would prefer to be alone? he says, as if it has suddenly dawned on him.

No, not necessarily, says Unnar, before I have a chance to reply.

Bishop Holub turns toward me.

Providing you agree . . . Although, naturally, I only know what I've read. As with the famous fog, he says, grinning.

I would have wanted him to leave, but now I have to agree to his continued presence. I had tried to persuade myself that Unnar's intention was simply to unburden himself to me—to me alone and no one else—and that it would be up to me whether or not to take matters further, but that fantasy has evaporated.

Bishop Holub is accustomed to being in charge. Now he looks at Unnar, as if to indicate that it is time for him to speak.

Unnar seems unprepared, although he has undoubtedly gone over this in his mind countless times. He clears his throat, lowers his head then looks at me.

Of course, this all happened a long time ago, he begins falteringly. And still that morning remains vivid in my memory. Perhaps, because I have never stopped thinking about it. Or about my years at the school, although I wish I could forget them.

He clears his throat again and takes a sip of coffee, before continuing.

For a long time I was unable to talk about that period. I always blamed myself. Apparently this is typical of children who have been victims of abuse.

The phrasing obviously comes from his discussions with the therapist who has been helping him, indeed his voice changes when he utters the words. The bishop glances at me, but I indicate that I am as bewildered as he.

Forgive me, says the bishop, but have you spoken about this before?

Unnar shakes his head.

No, I have never dared mention it to anyone.

Abuse, you say . . . Do you mean . . . ?

He doesn't need to finish the question, because the young man's expression makes the answer glaringly obvious.

The bishop frowns. I imagine that he is reflecting on the awkward situation this may put him in.

I was in knitting class, Unnar resumes. I was never any good at it. I remember waiting for Miss Stein to pick on me. The way she always did. No matter how hard I tried. There were three of us who she used to bully regularly, although I was the one she hit the most. Sometimes she would take me to Father August Frans. That was the worst punishment. The broom cupboard was heaven in comparison. I was free to let my mind wander. I was a bit of a dreamer, he adds, a smile playing on his lips.

I read a lot of comics. My father would bring them when he came home from sea. He was a steersman on a freighter, before he . . .

He falls silent, looks down for a moment then continues.

The text was in English, but I could follow the pictures. After he died, I almost never put them down.

I was particularly keen on Batman. He was my hero. I was thinking about him in the broom closet, remembering one of the stories, all of which I knew by heart. I think I can still recall some of them even now . . .

He pauses, seems to lose himself for a moment, then resumes.

I thought for a long time about what it was I actually saw. As opposed to what I imagined I saw. It was all jumbled up in my head. But I think I've succeeded, and that now I can finally see everything clearly. Bessi—my therapist—agrees. But it has been a lengthy process.

He looks at me.

That's why I wrote you the letter, Sister. Because I didn't tell them everything when we were sitting here with the detective twenty years ago. I wasn't trying to hide anything, I was just confused. For many years, I was confused.

I am keen to bring the meeting to an end, to tell him that the most important thing is that he feels better now, that he has found his place in life, and there is no need to talk about anything else. To dredge up the past, disturb his newfound peace of mind. The past will never return, I should point out, but his future is before him, and I am sure he should now be able to look ahead with optimism.

Are you a family man? I should ask, and then turn the conversation to his job, his life on the east coast, even the famous fog that Bishop Holub mentioned. But the words won't come, and I can barely move in my seat. I look at the coffee turning cold in my cup but haven't the appetite or the will to pick it up.

When you opened the door, I wet myself because I was terrified that you knew what I was thinking. I thought you could see how relieved I was when I realized that it was Father August Frans lying dead on the ground. But then you took me in your arms, and everything went silent. It was as if you had spread a warm blanket over me when I was so cold. That's how I felt. Exactly how I felt. And at last I understood everything they told us about Jesus, the comfort he's supposed to bring. At last I understood.

But I didn't tell you everything . . .

He clasps then unclasps his fingers, toys with the sleeves of his checked shirt. *You needn't do this*, I say to him in my head, *you needn't talk*. But he goes on, he says the words I have always feared would one day be uttered.

He wasn't alone . . .

Out of the corner of my eye, I see the bishop rise up slightly from his chair.

What do you mean? he asks.

Up in the tower. He wasn't alone.

The bishop looks at me, bewildered.

I wasn't trying to hide anything, Unnar resumes. It just took me so long to process everything. But now I'm sure. I can see it all much more clearly.

Bishop Holub leans forward in his chair, and I see from his expression that he has misgivings. Before he voices them, I say in a low voice:

Tell us what you saw.

The bishop sits back and waits for Unnar to speak.

I need to do this in the right sequence. I was thinking about Batman. That's why I got everything mixed up. Then I look up at the tower, and see him standing there, at the open window. My hero. Of course, I was startled, because deep down I knew I was imagining it. Deep down. But then I see him right there, and I feel he's looking at me and that he's about to fly down to me . . . And then he does, only his cape stays up in the open window, and it isn't Batman at all, but Father August Frans who hits the ground.

And he is just wearing his suit, his black suit. So I look up at the tower again, and I see a black cape flapping in the wind before it disappears.

I know it sounds a little confusing, but I am sure he wasn't alone.

Disappears where? the bishop asks.

I saw someone back away from the opening and then they just vanished.

Someone?

Yes, I don't know if it was a man or a woman. It could have been a priest, or a nun, or possibly a woman in a black dress or coat. I don't know. Nor do I know if that person pushed him or was trying to save him. All I remember is an outstretched arm . . .

Was it the headmaster's arm or . . . ? the bishop asks.

I don't know. It was snowing, and I couldn't see very well.

Are you sure about this? says the bishop.

He nods.

Yes, I'm sure.

And then I hear myself say, to my surprise and relief:

Has it ever occurred to you who that person might have been?

He looks down, clasping his fingers again. I can see that he has asked himself this question countless times, discussed it with his therapist, speculated, changed his mind, had misgivings, been absolutely sure—only to be assailed by doubt moments later.

I've had a few ideas, but nothing worth mentioning. I couldn't see well enough.

We sit for a while longer. Holub asks him a few trivial questions, to which Unnar gives clear answers, but he looks at me more than at the bishop.

I felt I had to reveal this, he says at last. About the abuse, and what I saw that morning. Otherwise I will never have closure, he adds.

We rise from our chairs, the bishop first. I have been wondering why Unnar felt such a strong need for me to be there, for he is no longer a little boy who lacks the courage to speak to the bishop alone. I have an idea about what the answer might be, as I sensed from the moment we sat down at the table that somehow he was comparing me to his memory, with the person he saw at the window twenty years ago. I saw it in his eyes, and now, as he comes over to say good-bye, I get the proof.

We are out in the hallway, the bishop's office to our left, the main door to our right. He clasps my hand, and when our eyes meet I see that he knows it was me.

He quickly lets go of my hand, embraces me instead, and whispers:

Thank you, Sister. You saved me.

And then he vanishes through the door, and all I can see is the rain falling slowly until the door closes by itself.

I AM SITTING IN THE CONSERVATORY AT THE GUESTHOUSE in Garðastræti looking out at the lawn. Shortly after lunch, much to everyone's surprise, the rain stopped and the sun came out, prompting some of the guests to take their coffee in the garden. I stayed inside, but I shall not deny that it cheered me to see them out in the sunshine. I felt somehow that with the sun an imaginary wall disappeared and shackles fell from my feet. No sooner had the first rays burst forth from the skies than a cloud lifted from the guests, both those who rose from their chairs to go outside, as well as us few who remained seated.

I contemplate the garden once more as I sip my coffee, and I have to admit that there is more to it than meets the eye; indeed, it is quite varied considering the location. The flower beds and shrubs are well placed and enjoy both sunshine and shelter from the wind, although a few of the trees are overly tall, creating unnecessary shade. However, there are a few stumps where some have been cut down, and I can't see that they should be missed.

After I got back from Bishop Holub's yesterday, I switched on my phone and discovered a long message from Sister Marie Joseph. In it, she explained the reason for her lengthy silence: George Harrison had gone missing and only been found minutes ago. She didn't say exactly when he ran off, but I assumed it must have been about two days ago, soon after she sent me her last text. She explained that the farmer nearby had finally spotted him up on the hill, all wet and bedraggled; it had been raining constantly since he went missing and had suddenly gotten cold. However, he was in good hands now, so I needn't worry. She hadn't wanted to bother me before he was found . . .

She apologized profusely for not having taken better care of him; however, I didn't blame her, in fact I was grateful that she had waited until now to tell me. All the same, I wondered what on earth he was doing in the hills, for we seldom walk there, except in spring, when I am building myself up after the winter.

She sent me a photograph of George Harrison and looking at it enabled me to forget about Unnar Grétarsson for a while. His words had kept echoing in my head, despite my efforts to thrust them aside, and I could still feel his embrace.

Bishop Holub had asked to have a word with me after Unnar had gone. Our exchange was brief. He told me a journalist had contacted his office recently to inquire about Father August Frans's alleged misdemeanors. After all this time, he remarked, adding that the journalist claimed to be in touch with a pupil who had been a victim. And now this, he said, and of course what emerged in your report. I don't see how we can possibly avoid facing these horrors.

However, he simply remarked that the poor man was still clearly struggling with ghosts from his past, and that it was impossible after all this time for us to separate fact from fantasy, especially when Unnar was barely able to do so himself.

Let us hope he finds his way in life, he said. Some people never recover.

In the photograph, George Harrison is lying beside the stove wrapped in a blanket. Beside him sits his empty bowl. I can tell that he is enjoying life, and I say to myself that it would be typical of him to repeat the escapade, if as a result he is pampered and spoiled for his misbehavior.

I miss him dreadfully, and the rose garden, the view from my cell, the calm mornings, the sunrise. The aroma of wet soil, and the closeness of the ground, the peace in solitude. And yet our reunion must wait a while, for I realized when I woke up this morning that my task is incomplete.

Páll answered on the third ring. The young man in reception helped me find his telephone number, and as luck would have it only two other people with the same name were listed in Reykjavík. Our exchange was brief, but he was very pleasant. Naturally, he was surprised to hear from me, but he sounded every bit as cheerful as when he came to fetch me from the bus station all those years ago. He asked whether I had plans tonight, and when I said no, he invited me to his house for dinner. I am to go there at seven.

I wonder if I should follow the example of the people in the garden, as the sun has stayed out longer than I anticipated. In fact, I've been expecting fair weather rain, because the clouds are still lingering, floating across the sun every now and then. But suddenly the sky clears, the clouds seem to be dispersing, and I see no reason not to get up and go out into the garden.

I feel energetic, even though I hardly slept last night. By the time I set aside Halla's letters, the dusk that makes a cursory appearance for good measure had lifted, and light was once again dancing around the room. That was when I decided to rent a car again and drive to Stykkishólmur, for I need to say good-bye to her before I leave. It can't be too difficult for me to locate her grave, and although I know full well that I will find only a freshly dug plot, where possibly a temporary cross has been planted, I am sure that there it will be easier for me to find the words to express what is in my heart.

I know now that I was loved. From here on, she will always be with me.

I walk out into the garden and sit down on a little bench next to the garden lupines and the foxglove. Plump, happy-looking bees are buzzing in the flower bed. When I got out of bed and drew the curtains, I decided to stop telling myself my life had been meaningless. So far today, I have succeeded, and I am confident that the clear skies will hold out.

I feel no remorse. That never changes, despite all my efforts, my discussions with myself, invoking and cursing God by turns. In my mind, I see him fall to the ground, and I never regret my actions, I never grab hold of him in my dreams to prevent him from falling. I never wake up in despair. And yet I frequently needle myself for not having acted out of compassion for his victims, or even because of a burning desire to stop him; yes, I torment myself constantly, accusing myself of simply having been unable to accept that he got the better of me.

Perhaps it's true. I hope not, but I don't know. Still, I feel no remorse.

I lean back on the bench. The bees are buzzing, and all of a sudden I realize how tired I am. God willing, if I close my eyes, I may succeed in forgetting myself for a while and perhaps even find myself in a dream where everything is just as it should be.

OLAF OLAFSSON was born in Reykjavík, Iceland, in 1962. He studied physics as a Wien scholar at Brandeis University. He is the author of five previous novels: *The Journey Home*, *Absolution*, *Walking into the Night*, *Restoration*, and *One Station Away*, and a story collection, *Valentines*. He was an executive vice president of Time Warner and lives in New York City with his wife and three children.